Beddington Manor

Beddington Manor

By

Kelly Haglund

Beddington Manor

Reviews

"For a while, I forgot this was fiction. I couldn't put it down." – Brolin Burke, long time friend.

"Every time I look in a mirror, I'll think about your book. You may have cured my vanity!" - Stella Wood, new fan.

"This book was a pleasure to read. It should be a movie." – Kerry Cooke, *Health wise* magazine editor.

Beddington Manor

Forward

Beddington Manor is an old folks home with a secret.

Tom Benson, reporter, sent to interview the oldest living American in the most remote corner of Montana, Johnny J Johnson. Mr. Johnson claims to be 122 years old.

Benson embarks on a search for the secret of long life. With the help of Emma Sorensen, he learns much more.

If you journey to Twodot Montana, and enter Beddington Manor, you will think twice before you look into another mirror for the rest of your hours on earth.

Beddington Manor

Disclaimer

**This book was written in the sense fun and
fantasy. Any names, places or circumstances that
reflect or replicate real people, places or
circumstances is pure coincidence.**

On either side of the mirror.

Beddington Manor

Dedication

This book is dedicated to my brother Douglas Haglund. Doug read the first draft of this book, corrected and circled all the mistakes with a smiley face and a big red X on each page.

Doug was my brother, mentor and best of all, friend.

He ran out of hours April 15th 2004.

1938-2004

Beddington Manor

Acknowledgements

A special thanks to all of my personal editors:
JoAnn Hayes
Barbara Lawhorn
Douglas Haglund

A very special thanks to my wife for putting up
with
All of my rants and raves for the duration.
Bev

A special thanks to my professional Editors:
Kate Baxter
Kerry Cooke
Debbie Malone

And of course to you for buying this book!
(add your name here)

Beddington Manor

Chapter One

I had the gift or maybe it was a curse. I knew things. Things I wasn't supposed to know. It was simple deductive reasoning. At least that's how I justified it in my mind. However, even I sometimes thought it was truly remarkable. Sometimes I knew the answers to questions that were yet to be asked. Some faces on the street or in a café seemed too familiar. Familiar enough for me to say hello to people I didn't know and call them by name. While just passing them on the street I would say 'good morning' and say their name and simply walk past them without giving it another thought. It would generally catch them off guard. Most would just say hi and go on. However, every now and then one would stop and turn around and take a double take. A few have even stopped and engaged me in a quick Q and A.

"Do I know you?" they would say. The first time it happened, I surprised myself and told the bystander we must have met somewhere, without really knowing where or when. As it happened over and over, I began to consciously suppress my knowledge on the street.

Taking my 'problem' to a professional, they all had suppositions. Psychic was the term they used.

That was a catch-all the big brains used when they couldn't really explain the anomaly.

I don't really remember when it all started, but I do remember how. It seems it all started with my dreams. Dreams I remembered, not the trip so much, but always the substance.

So here I am again, looking through a window, knowing it's happening again and can't do a thing to stop it. I can't remember how I got here and again I'm not even sure where here is. Not the deductive reasoning I was hoping for. I wondered, if you think you're having a dream while you're having a dream, is it a dream or is it real? I turned my head to the left to see a hallway of windows that went on as far as I could see. In front of each window stood a ghostly image, clothed in silver. They were starring into the windows, I turned to the right to see the same. I again looked into the window in front of me to see the arduous scene. My window was smaller than most of the rest. Eye level and barely large enough to see the goings on. My view was distorted some and yet I could see a building getting smaller and changing from a mansion to a dilapidated shell. The woman standing in front of the building began to fade, I watched without saying a word. I tried to reach out, but couldn't move. I tried to speak, but was muted. I was riveted to my place.

It was no one I knew, it was somewhere I'd never been, but it *was* someone. . . and it *was* somewhere . . . familiar.

I felt powerless as the observer, unable to interact with my surroundings.

I saw a shadow now where the woman was standing just seconds ago. The next view was a hand reaching for and adjusting the window. Only eyes were visible now and they were fixed on me. We stared at each other for what seemed like hours, his eyes to mine.

Then, within the blink of an eye I was whisked away to another window. I saw a beautiful woman brushing her hair, checking her makeup. She looked to be around forty, with long auburn hair, green eyes and a face, smooth as glass. She wore black slacks, a silk blouse and one of those sweater coats. Diamond earrings, a Rolex and a classy single diamond floating on a gold chain. She checked the lipstick on her teeth, wiped it off, then turned away from me and left my line of vision.

Looking through the window, I was left staring at an empty room. I looked every direction only to see the room. My peripheral vision caught people moving all around me. I turned my head to see the figures moving, walking and glancing back at me, however it was all done in silence, like a dream but...

I turned and again in a blink, I was back in my reality, back in my shower, back into my morning routine. No longer in the black hallway. I was home.

I glanced across the bathroom to the mirror. Seeing myself in the shower was a surprise. I didn't remember waking, turning on the shower or even getting in. I recalled my dream and knew something big was on the horizon. It always started this way, a vision, a new assignment and me, always trying to figure it out.

I remembered *some* dreams better than others. Sometimes I came up with the answer or solution without knowing where it came from.

Sometimes I couldn't make the call. The visions were not of my choosing. They came, not on request but randomly and with no pattern. I've learned to accept the dreams or visions for what they were. Just dreams. The things I saw may not have been set. I could do nothing to stop the action from happening in my dreams and because of that, I convinced myself these visions were just maybes.

Chapter Two

I knew my boss was looking for me. I had just returned to my office in Denver from an assignment that took me to Louisiana and Florida, and my article on quicksand fatalities in the South was overdue.

Jack Shyrer was on the warpath. He seemed to always be on the warpath, very excitable and generally hostile. He started the Of Interest magazine sixteen years ago with nothing more than an idea that people would read the newspaper and hunger for more information.

Since newspapers were on deadline, they didn't always get all the facts before they went to press. Each month, 'Of Interest' magazine published stories of current events from all over the world. We covered everything from royal weddings to Hollywood scandals. We covered all-sized events, from the first cloned sheep to Mid-East turmoil. I've personally covered the last space shuttle takeoff, Jell-O recipe bake-off contests, and the President's inaugural ball. Now Of Interest is printed in twenty languages and sent all over the world.

Jack built the magazine by taking risks. He received newspapers countrywide and news tips came in from around the world. He would send reporters anywhere to cover what he perceived to be of interest. He had deadlines. Jack always had deadlines.

I, on the other hand, wanted to get all of the information. It always took time to assemble an article to make it just right. I figured if it didn't get into this month's issue, it could always go into next month's. We were not competing with the newspapers anymore. That's one of the reasons I joined Jack and his team.

I was like any other reporter who had been doing the same job for twenty years. I still had a mortgage, a car payment, and a daughter in college. I had worked for the high school newspaper when I was seventeen and the college paper all four years I was at Colorado State University. I married my high school sweetheart, the love of my life... We were both natives to Denver. We had our first son, Tommy Jr., during our first year in College. Our next boy, Joseph, named after his grandfather, came during my senior year of school. Our baby Dempsey was the last of the brood. My wife quit school to stay home with our kids. I took a night job all through school, and between that and college loans, we managed to get by.

I wanted to be a reporter so my major in school was journalism. During my senior year of college, I applied to both of the major papers in Denver and some of the weeklies. The Denver Post interviewed all applicants from college who had a 4.0 average, hiring about 2 or 3 college grads per year. That included me. I worked for the Denver Post for twenty years. The same day I graduated from school I started as a copy boy, and after only four months I moved into the printing room and learned to set type.

After my day at the paper, I would go out on assignment with one of the reporters. I learned exactly what they did, how they found their stories and manipulated the sources which is what they called anyone they talked to. If anyone ever asked where they received their information, the reporters would always just say 'a reliable source.' After a while I moved up to a junior reporter. I was still in the office, but I was working with a real reporter and learning to put the stories together. I wanted to get into the field, so I took the next upgrade to the position of a photographer. In my off hours, I sat in my car and listened to the police radio.

As soon as I heard something that sounded newsworthy, I sped to the scene and took pictures, always hoping I'd have something we could use in the paper.

Each time there was an opening for reporter, I put in my bid. I knew each new job was a step up and a new opportunity. I finally made it. I thought to be a reporter was more than just regurgitating the news. I was proud to be a reporter. It was like being paid to tell the truth about other people. In this profession, you're always looking for the next story, the next event, sometimes the next tragedy. After twenty years of deadlines, limitations of freedom and the paper being sued for slander every other day, I thought it might be smart to move to another venue.

For the past four years I've been working for this international magazine. Jack Shyrer lured me away from the Post with promises of exotic travel, interesting stories to work on and a higher quality of life. The increase in compensation didn't hurt either.

Working with Jack proved to be a challenge. He wanted everyone to know he was in charge. He always talked loud and slow when he was trying to make a point, as if the person he was talking to was either deaf or just couldn't understand. Jack could be very direct.

He would, glare over the tops of his reading glasses, his tie loosened, and declare that "Of Interest magazine had never missed a deadline and is not about to today."

I always thought, to do an article right, you needed all of the facts. Give the readers all the information and let them judge the validity of the story. Show both sides of any controversy, and take your lumps. If the public hated it, they could buy some other magazine. That was easy for me, it wasn't my magazine. The fact was, the public loved this magazine. Sales figures backed this up.

The public seemed to eat up everything we covered. They laughed at the funny things, like the man who thought he was Spiderman and decided to climb the side of a state capitol. He only climbed buildings where he figured he would be caught.

"No sense in climbing something that no one ever knew I climbed," he shouted and smiled as he was led off in handcuffs.

Some stories dominated our magazine for months. We were all so surprised by the interest from the foreign press. Even though most of the articles were about events in the United States, some were focused on Europe and Asia. The US readers enjoyed articles from abroad as well.

I thought I was ready for Jack today. When he found me, he just gave me the look. I headed directly to his office with him on my heels.

"I know my article is late. I've already talked to the typesetters, and they said I have three more hours."

Jack raised his hand to halt my excuses and said, "Close the door."

"Close the door?" I repeated. Jack stared at me until I followed his command. Once the door was closed Jack handed me the newspaper. I read the headline CORPORATE MERGERS ABOUND.

"Yeah, so what?" I asked.

"Not that," he said. "Look at the article I circled on the back page." I turned the paper over and in the bottom left corner, saw a quick report headlined "The Oldest Living Man in America." The filler just said "Congratulations to Johnny J. Johnson, the oldest living man in America. Celebrating his 100 and counting years alive. Surely the oldest man alive." To the left of the small filler, there was a picture of an old white haired gentleman. I looked up to see Jack staring at me.

Again I said, "Yeah, so what?"

Jack seemed to look right through me. "Why didn't they put his age in there but still claimed that he's the oldest living man in America? Why didn't they say where this guy lived? Why did they put this in our paper? Does he live here in Denver?"

I just sat there, dumbfounded. Why was my boss going on about some old guy instead of complaining about my quicksand fatality article being so late?

"I'm very curious about this," Jack went on. He began pacing the floor. "We need to know more about this Johnny J. Johnson, who he is, who he was, why he's still alive, you know, all the skinny. How about his wife, kids, grandkids? Where is he now? All the stuff of interest. Call the paper, you still have some contacts there, right?" Jack sat back down and drew another breath, removed his glasses. "Tom, I want you to find out!" I let out a groan.

"Oh Jack, I'm still working on that drive-by from last week. Not to mention the piece I owe the typesetters."

Jack raised his stop-talking hand to me and said, "You'll have that quicksand piece done within your three-hour reprieve, and Faye Hill can cover the drive-by, she can handle that." I raised an eyebrow. He continued to stare into me. Then that uncomfortable silence for all of twenty seconds.

"It's settled then, you'll start on this in the morning." I began to squawk again, but Jack just put his hand up again and waved me out of his office.

Putting his glasses on and glaring at me over the top, he said slowly, "Just interview the guy, find out how old he is, have it ready for our next issue. You can fax in your report, so it'll be here before you are." As I looked up from the newspaper, Jack was just smiling at me with that big fake grin that said, "Go do it."

I walked out muttering, "Do you know how many Johnny Johnson's there are in Denver?" I glanced back to see Jack holding another folded newspaper in one hand and a picture frame that had been on his desk in the other.

Until now, I'd felt pretty sure that I'd be in town for awhile. I'd just returned from two months in Florida and Louisiana where fourteen quicksand drownings had been reported this year. Actually you suffocate in quicksand, you don't drown. Last year there were only three deaths and the year before that, two. I was glad to return to the arid climate of Denver. August and September are the most humid months down south.

Back at my desk I started making phone calls. I loved my boys but Dempsey's was the only picture on my desk, It was really all I had room for. I had four In baskets and one out basket, full of tips and leads to stories I'd already written. I had a nail spindle stacked with pink 'while you were out' notices. Calls I needed to return. I went through my messages as I made the calls.

I located my old pal Gil, at the Post. He told me that at last count there were 392 people working at the Post, and he had no idea who had written the article. Maybe he could pull up the feed. The Feed was the background of each story, the reporter who wrote it, and all the notes the reporter entered into the database. When I asked for the specifics on Johnny Johnson,

Gil just said "Maybe."

I told him that our magazine was giving this old man some kind of award. I acted non-chalant about it all, so he nor the Post would be interested in doing a follow-up to their original story. It may have turned into nothing, however I knew it was something I wanted to explore without competition. He said it would cost me more than some lame award to get the information. Gil misunderstood and thought he was going to receive the award, I didn't correct him but instead, just said I would be glad to owe him.

Within the hour Gil called back. "The information came in from an e-mail that said this Johnson guy was celebrating his 122nd birthday. His great granddaughter said she wanted to congratulate her great granddad and wanted it in the paper so she could show him. As far as I know, no one verified it so we just put it in one of the back pages of the daily and didn't use his age because, like I said, no one verified it."

"What about the great granddaughter," I knew he may not give up the information. Most 'rags' didn't divulge their source. But Gil and I went way back. When I was a senior reporter for the Post, Gil was one of the new copy boys.

I got pretty excited when Gil said, "Now you didn't hear this from me." I grabbed a pen from my pocket and wrote down kateslybeck@true.com. Now I was looking for two people, Johnny J. Johnson and Kate Slybeck or Lybeck or maybe just Beck. I became a little more interested now, pondering the beginning of a mystery. To be a good investigative reporter, you have to be a hunter. Good reporters are great detectives.

Chapter Three

The next morning, I stopped first at the Bureau of Records, where all public records are kept in some giant computer. We don't really know how it works, it just does. Here I could check on both Kate and Mr. Johnson at the same time. I smiled and showed my ID to the young clerk, who said,

"Tom Benson, super sleuth, hard at it again, huh Tom?"

I winked and said, "Hi Wendy" as I walked past the front counter and sat at the first available computer terminal. When I typed in John Johnson I got 497 matches.

INPUT: <u>John J Johnson</u>
OUTPUT: 230 matches.

INPUT: <u>Johnny</u> J. Johnson

OUTPUT: 54 matches.

I printed the info.

"What are the chances?" I said half aloud. I did the same thing for Kate Beck with no matches. I input Kate Lybeck and still no matches then I entered Kate Slybeck and bingo, 1 match found. I took the print.

Name: Kate Slybeck
Address: 924 Columbine Rd
                    Denver, Colorado
Phone; 303-989-9220
Occupation   Retired

If she was retired, maybe she could have a grandfather who was a hundred. I knew I needed to talk to this Slybeck person before checking the usual sources like the power company, the phone company, bureau of licenses and department of transportation for a one in fifty-four chances that Johnny J. Johnson might be in their records.

Back at my office, I called Kate Slybeck throughout the day, to be continually connected to an answering machine. I left several messages and just hung up on the other unanswered calls. I sent an e-mail to kateslybeck@true.com explaining what I wanted, or at least what I thought I could tell her.

All I really wanted to do was talk to her great grandfather. I started going through my list of Johnny Johnson's. I figured I could eliminate any of them that were younger than one hundred. That only left four. I started calling the telephone numbers listed in the files. Two of the numbers had been disconnected, and the other two, well, only had bad news about John J Johnson. They had both passed away within the last year. I was back to square one, finding Kate Slybeck.

I spent the rest of the day searching the Internet, looking at everything from the history files of Denver to the woman in South Africa who was reported to be 107 last month. I cleared my e-mail back up. I returned a number of calls that had piled up on my desk. At 5:00 I took all the Johnson files and headed home.

After dinner I tried Kate again. She answered the phone. "Hello."

"Hello," I said, surprised. "This is Tom Benson, A reporter with the Of Interest magazine. I saw the article in the Post about your great grandfather."

"Yes." she said unimpressed.

I continued, "Would it be possible to talk to him?"

"I just took him home." She said. "He's not here."

"I noticed that in the paper, it didn't mention his age," I said.

"Yes, I don't remember if I gave that to the paper, I told them he was the oldest man alive. I was just glad they printed the birthday notice. It really made his day." Warming just a bit.

I asked, "Could we meet tomorrow and maybe talk about your great grandfather?"

"Are you going to do a story on my great grandpa?" she asked.

"I would like to talk to your great grandfather if that's possible. Sometimes we catch something from the local paper that may have broader appeal. I think this could be one of those stories. How old did you say he was?"

"Just turned 122." Was the response. Before I could answer, she added, "Do you know where the Roasters coffee house is?"

"Yes, of course."

She went on, "Does ten o'clock work for you?"

"That would be great." I said.

The Roasters Coffeehouse was a small place that only the locals knew about and frequented. I arrived thirty minutes early and it occurred to me that I had no idea what Kate Slybeck looked like. I was looking for a retired woman. Retired from what, I had no idea, but her file said she was retired. I was hoping I could figure out who she was when she walked in. A woman arrived just five minutes before ten, ordered a cup of coffee and walked directly over to my table and asked

"Tom Benson?" I stood up, put my hand out to shake hers.

"You must be Kate." She shook my hand and I said, "Thanks for meeting with me on such short notice." Kate looked to be around forty, with long auburn hair, green eyes and a face, smooth as glass. She looked like she just stepped out of a fashion magazine. She was dressed in black slacks, a silk blouse and one of those sweater coats. The blouse and sweater coat were color coordinated. She wore the coat open with the belt hanging from the loops. Diamond earrings, a Rolex and a classy single diamond floating on a gold necklace rounded out her stylish persona. She was one of those people I felt like I knew. Something about her was very familiar.

A quick flashback hit me, of seeing her through a window wiping the lipstick off of her teeth. Walking away from me, stopping at the door turning back and giving me a wink and a little smile.

I learned a long time ago to suppress those feelings and carry on with the matters at hand. I also knew it wasn't the years you needed for retirement, it's the money. And it looked like she had plenty. We didn't talk about it, but I could tell she had it.

"I guess you had some questions about my grandfather," Kate questioned. "Well really he's not my grandfather, my grandfather died eight years ago. Johnny Johnson is my Dad's great Grandfather. We all just call him Grandpa." I was trying to pay attention to each word and yet my mind wandered as I was trying to figure how many generations she had just whipped through.

"Your Dad's great Grandfather? How old did you say he was? That would be four or five generations of the Johnson clan? That's remarkable." I guess I looked a little doubtful to Kate.

"A lot of people get that look on their face when I tell them how old grandpa is. Grandpa turned 122 this year. I know it sounds unreal, but he just keeps going and stays busy up at the home. He says he found the *secret*, whatever that is. He's not getting around like he used to, but he does okay. We all just laugh and say he's just to ornery to die. Of course he's just about the nicest man you could ever meet." I must have looked like I was still trying to do the figures in my head because Kate stopped talking. After a minute I said,

"That means your Grandpa was born in 1880? The secret?" I looked up from my notepad. "Secret?" I said again. Kate confirmed my comment about his birth year, continued to drink her coffee. I was still thinking when I asked,

"Could I meet with him this afternoon?"

Kate let out a quick laugh, "I don't think so. I mean, it might be possible if he was here in town. He doesn't live here. He lives in Montana. Twodot, Montana. He lives in a retirement home, Beddington Manor. He loves it up there. I've tried to get him to spend more time here with me, and he visits about once a year. He won't fly, so I pick him up and I take him home when he's had enough." The server came over to refill our cups. She asked if we needed anything else and left our bill on the table.

Kate went on, "Beddington isn't like other retirement homes. First off, it's almost impossible to get in. I guess they have a waiting list."

Kate opened her purse and pulled out a small round compact, opened it and proceeded to touch up her cheek, pulled a lipstick tube and touched up her lips. She took a napkin and wiped it a little lipstick from her teeth. I simply watched. When she noticed me staring she looked up from her mirror and said,

"I can give you the number."...

Chapter Four

I was on the phone as soon as I hit the front door. I was explaining to the Curator of Beddington Manor in Twodot, Montana that our magazine would like to interview the oldest living American, so I needed access into his old folks home. The man immediately corrected me.

"We prefer it to be called Beddington Manor or at the very least, retirement home, but never Old Folks Home," he said. He continued to tell me that I would probably not be able to interview Mr. Johnson due to the strict rules of the house.

"Basically it is family only, that are allowed in to see their loved ones. All others need an appointment."

I asked, "How do I get an appointment?"

"You would need to speak directly to the resident or have the family's permission."

"May I speak to Mr. Johnson?" I asked.

"Mr. Johnson doesn't have a phone and residents are not allowed to use mine. You know, house rules." The phone went dead. I made another call to Kate Slybeck hoping to get the permission the Curator said I needed. She had already granted me the permission verbally, but I was sure I would need something in writing. Each call was again answered by her recorder. I left another e-mail requesting written confirmation of permission to interview her great grandfather.

I made plans to fly to Montana the next day and find a way into the Manor. I had always been able to get through the toughest layers of security and one misguided curator of an old folks home was certainly no match for me.

I needed to look up an old friend, Barb Hornwal at the National Hall of Records. Barb always helped me when I worked for the Post. She was a good resource and would do almost anything for a little chocolate. All of the information she provided was always public record, but she knew where to look. I told her of my need for some information on a senior citizen, and she was more than willing to help. I began to tell her of how interesting this assignment was becoming, she didn't really care. She nodded a few times, and disappeared into the records room. She came back with the file.

"I have John J. Johnson's file. If you wait a little while I can copy it or I can upload all of the information to your computer."

"Of course, I'll wait." I said.

I headed for home with a folder in my hand and a cherry cordial still on my breath. Barb had shared her newly acquired chocolates with me. I planned to start my quest for the interview of Johnny J. Johnson the next day. When I arrived at home, I checked my e-mail. I had received nothing from Kate Slybeck. I sent another e-mail to ask that she inform the curator of Beddington of her approval for me to meet with her Great grandfather. I downloaded some information Barb sent to me that I didn't have before I left the Hall of Records, and began to look over each file.

In the folder was a picture, probably taken forty or fifty years ago, I thought to myself. I went through the file to find copies of his records, with all the usual items, such as school report cards, a police record, One arrest when he was thirty for aggravated assault. "Oh it seems Johnny was a bad boy huh?" I said out loud. Other forms, that were in the folders included copies of some of his diplomas. Johnny J. Johnson was a doctor.

Then I noticed no birth certificate. Instead, there was a page that looked like the inside cover of a book.

Child # 9
Name   Sara Johnson
Sex   Female
Weight   8lbs. 0 oz.
Length   20.0 inches
Date   June 24 1880
Child #10
NAME Johnathan James Johnson
Sex   Male
Weight 8lbs 3 oz.

Length 21.5 inches
Date   March 4, 1884
Child #11
Name   Jerry Lynn Johnson
Sex   Male
Weight 5lbs. 13 oz.
Length 19.5 inches
Date   February 1 1886

The next file was the picture of a Bible. This was the way people used to document childbirth in those days. That would indeed make him a hundred and twenty two years old, just as his grand daughter had said. That would be impossible. "No way, no no way." This guy should be dead by now. I looked again at the picture of Johnny Johnson; the picture itself was obviously fifty or more years old. When I turned the picture over it said 1990. I turned it again to view the picture. I was sure the person in this photo was not a hundred and twelve years old. I went back over some of the other documents in the folder. The more I looked, the more confusing it became. The very last file said:

Last know address: Denver Colorado.

Chapter Five

Helena Montana was the closest airport to Twodot. It was about 120 miles between the two. It was just a two-hour drive, so I would have plenty of time to analyze all of the things I had learned in the last few days. The reasonable explanation could have been some kind of typing error or maybe one of his kids was passing himself off for John Sr. Of course, if it was all true and he was still living, I had to wonder what the secret that Kate mentioned was. And why in Twodot? Wasn't this about the most remote area he could find?

I planned to stop at the next town and have some lunch. A road sign read "Paradise next exit". Even though I knew I only had about 40 or 50 miles

left before Twodot, I had many things to prepare
before my interview with Mr. Johnson. I figured I
should eat now and take care of business as soon as I
hit town.

Paradise was larger than I expected. It had a
number of restaurants and fast food places. One of the
billboards on the highway advertised affordable
housing, which probably meant it had plenty of empty
rooms and was only 60 miles from the college in
Central Montana. As I turned off the Highway into
town, I decided on Winn's Café and Diner on Main
street.

As I entered Winn's, I was able to seat myself
immediately. Winn's was like the old time cafés. A
long counter with an old time soda fountain machine
and six tables for the customers to relax and enjoy
their meal. The tables were the old style, like back in
the 50's, all yellow marbled tops with chrome legs.
The chair upholstery matched the tops of the table,
with chrome frames to match the table legs.

There were a few people in the cafe, eating
breakfast. I generally ate breakfast at five or six in the
morning, sometimes light and sometime not, so by
10:30 a.m. I was ready for lunch. I always tried to
hold off until 11, but could eat lunch almost anytime. I
ordered my usual. I could tell how good any café was
by the way they made their club sandwich.

As I was finishing my lunch, the waitress, a
young 20-year-old with a bouncing pony tail, still
chewing gum and thinking she was a kid, dropped off
my check at the table. I looked up and asked. "What
do you know about the Beddington house?"

She gave me a blank stare and said, "You
mean Beddington Manor?"

I nodded, adding "Twodot."

The waitress said she thought Twodot was a ghost town and that hardly anyone lived up there anymore. I was a little surprised at the thought of Twodot being a ghost town. My research had shown Twodot's population to be over 5,000 residents.

I finished my drink and went to the counter to pay the bill. The old man behind the cash register looked up at me and said, "My mom's up there."

Surprised, I asked "Beddington?"

"Yeah, the old gal is still hanging on, too mean to die, I reckon."

I laughed and asked, "Really?" He looked at me like I had insulted him. Of course it was okay for him to say it, but no one else should be saying his mother was a mean old gal.

I immediately began to interview him. It was like a switch that went on in me. I was always on the case, always on the story. "What's her name? How longs she been up there? How often do you see her? How old is she?" I went on. It seemed like once I started asking questions, I couldn't stop. This was a bad habit I had learned while trying to interview people who were less than cooperative. For the poor people who were more hospitable, I'm sure it felt like an attack. They generally overlooked my aggressive approach because they wanted to tell their story. I think most people just like talking and if anyone ever showed an interest in what they had to say, well, they opened right up. The uncooperative people, or the ones that didn't like to talk, always had something to hide. The man behind the counter blew off my battery of questions, I'm sure due to his age and wisdom.

As he was counting back my change, he said, "She's been up there for 30 years or so. I get up there to see her as often as I can. She's one of the young ones, only 102."

I asked, "One of the young ones? How many folks are up there?"

"Forty or Fifty, I guess, maybe more," the old man said. "Anyway, if you see her tell her hi from Dale."

"Her name?" I asked again.

He smiled and glanced around like he was telling me a secret or something. "Her name is Catherine, Catherine Banks."

I said I would happy to pass on Dale's greeting and waved on my way out the door.

Chapter Six

I hadn't counted on dirt roads for the last 30 miles, but due to a detour on the main road, dirt roads were the only option and I arrived in Twodot exhausted. Twodot was not as small as Miss chewing gum had portrayed. It had a hotel, not the Hilton, but a hotel just the same. The main street was paved and lined with many businesses, shops and even a couple of restaurants. The hotel had a main lobby and the man behind the check-in desk was wearing a uniform.

Casual, but a uniform with the name of the Twodot Hotel stenciled on the shirt.

I checked in, went to my room and sat down for a ten minute rest. I felt maybe I could stop vibrating for a few minutes before I went to locate the Beddington Manor.

The next morning, I awoke to find myself still in the clothes from the previous day. Disgusted, I figured it was morning and I better get going. Thirty minutes later I was in the hotel lobby looking for breakfast. The desk clerk said the best place in town for breakfast was the cafe just down the street a block. "What's the name of the café?" I asked.

The clerk hardly looked up from what he was doing and just said, "The Café."

I walked out of the hotel and headed to the café. You could tell this café was built when times were good. It was built in a U shape, with the counter across the front of the building and a wing on both sides of the entrance. Booths ran along both sides of the main counter and tables down the middle of each wing. The sign at the front said seat yourself. I took a middle booth on the left so I could see the street and the kitchen.

While eating my two eggs over easy with hash browns and sausage, I mentioned Beddington to the waitress. The waitress said her grandmother was up there.

I asked. "How often do you get to see her?" She responded. "Daily."

"How old is your grandma?" I asked. When she told me, I about choked in disbelief.

"105."

She saw my reaction, and must have read my mind, "They're all old up there," she said, "Do you have somebody up there?"

I was thinking about what she has just revealed. I already knew about Mr. Johnson and Catherine Banks both being over a hundred, and now there was another person over a hundred?

"Well, do ya?"

I kind of jumped at her sharp tone. "Ah, no, well… not family exactly. I just need to talk to one of the patients."

"Patients" she said, "Hell mister, they're not patients."

She walked away with the coffeepot in her hand and laughing. "Patients" she said again with her back to me. She turned back around and looked at me and said, "You know, you won't get in. Right?"

"What, what, hey wait a minute. What do ya mean I won't get in?" I said as I was jumping out of my seat, following her back to the main counter. "God, it's only an old folks home, isn't it?" She picked up a clean mug and poured another cup of coffee for me.

She said, "No, Mister, its Beddington Manor" like I was suppose to know what that meant. "You know, Walter Beddington?" She looked at me like I was from another planet. "You've never heard of Walter Beddington, have you? Beddington Manor, up the hill there was built by Walter. He used to own almost everything in this town at one time. I guess he practically built this town. In fact, it used to be called Beddington a long time ago." One of the other customers was trying to gain her attention and maybe get a little more coffee.

She said, "Have a seat, I'll be right back." She went to refill the caffeine-deprived regular with another cup. She came back and asked what I was going to do up at Beddington.

I said, "I came up to interview a Mr. Johnson. He is supposed to be the oldest living man in America." She was distracted again by the cook and she again excused herself and delivered the breakfast to one of the other customers in the cafe. When she returned to the counter, she said. "Basically the only way you can get in is if you have a relative up there. Are you a relative of Johnson's?"

I told her I represented the Of Interest magazine and I was here just to talk to Johnson.

Two more customers came in, and once again, she walked away to take care of business by seating the new customers. She gave them a menu and came back to get some water for them. She took their order, walked by me and placed their order on the pass through window to the kitchen. She turned around and continued, "What paper did you say you were from?"

"The Of Interest magazine." I replied.

"We really can't talk here." She said. The door to the Café opened again, two more people walked in.

"Could we talk later? I'd really like to know more. How long have you lived here?" I asked. She smiled at me, and then walked over to the Café entry and greeted the two guys that had just walked in. She motioned to an empty table. She came back to retrieve some more water.

She stopped and got a little closer to me and sort of whispered, "Meet me here after six and we'll talk about the Beddington Manor." I looked around to see if anyone was trying to listen to our conversation. I summized that they were not.

"Okay," I said and went up to the cash register to pay my bill. I left the café, more than a little confused. Here was a woman, whom I didn't know, that was willing to tell me all about the town's old folks home.

I headed back to my room for my briefcase and notes so I would be somewhat prepared to talk to Mr. Johnson. Secrets or no secrets, I was still going to talk to him today.

Chapter Seven

I arrived at the Beddington Manor at 10 a.m. Clearly, this was the grandest building in the town. It didn't seem to belong here. It was only six blocks from town, and yet it looked like it was a southern mansion from the Civil War days. It had two giant columns on the porch, which ran the full length across the front of the building and down one side all the way to the back. The whole house or manor was on a hill overlooking the town. I guessed it was probably built on this location for that very reason. Walter Beddingtons' name was over the entrance. The manor looked to be two floors with a giant dome in the center of the roof. It had twelve windows down both sides of the building on each floor. As I stood on the street corner and gazed at the Manor, I realized I was staring and quickly turned to see if anyone was watching me. There was no one on the porch of the Manor, so I headed up the stairs and into the front lobby. A man met me before I could even get to the counter. He appeared to be in his mid 50s. He was about 6 foot 5 with jet black, slicked back hair. This man cast a big shadow. He had a protruding brow which jutted out as he tilted his head forward to look down to me. He towered above with no sign of welcome. He had an attitude and displayed it well.

Even with something as harmless as "Can I help you?" In his deepest, darkest voice. I just stammered.

"I have an appointment, I mean a meeting, no I mean, a, ah, an appointment with Mr. Johnson, Mr. John Johnson." He looked at me and cocked his head to one side, paused for what seemed like an eternity and finally said "I highly doubt that.

Who made the appointment and when was it made?"

He paused, waiting for an answer, standing like a guard with his piercing eyes connected directly to mine. I was about to speak when he added, "And who was it made with?" He was almost barking at me.

"I actually talked to a Mr. Learchman just a couple of days ago."

He interrupted again and said, "I'm Learchman."

"Oh Hi. Ah, yes, well, I talked to *you* and I thought it was all arranged to talk to Mr. Johnson today." He continued to look through me, not saying anything until he could tell I was completely uncomfortable. I added "I also talked to Kate Slybeck, Mr. Johnson's granddaughter. Mrs. Slybeck said it was okay for me to talk to her grandfather."

Mr. Learchman said, "Well, that's not how it's done." He said he would need a letter or a phone call from Mrs. Slybeck before I could talk to anyone. He told me to sit down, pointing to the waiting area sofa. He walked back to the front desk and made a call. While he was on the phone, he was typing on his computer.

I took a seat, picked up a magazine and pretended to look at it. I subtly looked around, trying to soak it all in.

Beddington Manor somehow looked bigger on the inside than on the outside. As grand as it was on the outside, the inside was even better. The hallways seemed endless. Even the windows seemed to be different on the inside. The ceilings were at least 12 feet high. From my seat, I could see the grand staircase that went to the next floor. Just to the left of the grand staircase was a smaller doorway that I assumed went to the basement. I wondered how these old folks got up and down all of those stairs. There were a couple of people talking as they were walking down the hall. They appeared to be discussing one of the residents. I figured they must be the Doctors or some kind of Medical staff. They were wearing long white coats and carrying clipboards or journals or some papers. I waved to them, they waved back, looked at each other, chuckled and continued on down the hall away from me. I wanted to charge ahead and talk to them, but just then I could see Mr. Learchman walking back to me. I stood up.

Mr. Learchman came back to me and said abruptly and with no explanation, "You'll have to come back tomorrow."

I said, "I'll have Kate call you to give you the okay. I'll call her and say it's ..." My voice trailed off.

He maintained his stoic expression and just escorted me to the front door.

I stalled for some extra time, hoping to get some additional information from him, "This sure is a great old building, when was it built?" He opened the front door saying nothing. He ushered me to the outside and I tried again. "And built by?"

Mr. Learchman said only "Beddington." He pointed to the sign above. I was already on the porch, I glanced up to the sign that said Beddington.

I started to ask, "Does this town have a library?" He closed the door before I could get the entire question out. When I looked back through the door window, I could see Mr. Learchman heading back to his post at the front counter. I already knew there was not a library within a hundred miles, but it might have been nice to talk to Learchman a little longer. I'm sure he is full of information.

I stopped on my way down the front stairs and to make a note in my notebook: WALTER BEDDINGTON, BEDDINGTON MANOR. CHECK ON WILLIAM LEARCHMAN. Tucking the note away, I thought I had plenty of homework to do and was headed to the hotel to do a little research on the computer. As I began to walk away, I glanced back at the old folks home and noticed the windows again, I couldn't figure it out, but I knew they were different on the inside. I figured I must have been seeing things. Then I noticed someone watching me from one of the windows on the second floor. I couldn't make it out, but I was sure he or she was looking right at me. I looked at the window for a minute, glanced away and then the figure was gone. I turned and walked back to town and to my hotel.

Chapter Eight

The hotel room was extremely nice for being in such a small town. As you entered the room, it had the scent of freshness. To the left of the doorway was the refreshment center, a refrigerator, a microwave oven, and a sink. To the right of the doorway was a small by elegant living area, a couch and chair and TV. A table and a two chairs set close to the window. The view out the window was Main street. A hallway led to the sleeping quarters, a bed, a small dresser and of course a closet. The connecting bathroom had a claw foot bathtub, a large vanity and a mirror from the vanity to the ceiling, the width of the room.

I set up my laptop and plugged into the Internet. I had a number of messages from Shyrer. He asked if I had made contact and wanted a current status update of the story. I sent a reply to let him know the story was coming along just fine and I said I would keep the editor informed as to what was happening.

I sent another e-mail off to Kate Slybeck. I asked her to call Mr. Learchman and to give the okay for me to talk with her grandfather. I told her Mr. Learchman would not even let me into the Manor without her okay. I asked that she CC me on the e-mail. It was a little curious as to why she was not responding. I made a note to call her to touch base with her again. Next I pulled up a search engine and typed in Walter Beddington. During the next few hours, I learned that Walter Beddington was born in New York and moved to Montana to get away from the crowds. That happened back in 1880. He was a homesteader, sometimes called a squatter. He came to this area and put up a fence. Back in 1880, every person could receive 840 acres from the government, just for coming to the West. Walter actually fenced off 5000 acres of land. By the time the government knew what he had done, he had already been here a year and they couldn't do a thing about it. He discovered gold in the nearby hills, and that brought others to the area. He talked a Doctor into coming from Denver, some builders from New York, a lawyer and his family came from Chicago. He contacted schoolteachers, bankers, even a newspaper editor from Virginia. Eventually a town was born, the town of Beddington. Walter built an empire.

He and a few others built most of the buildings and owned most of the businesses. He figured he would eventually own the capital of Montana. I found a great article about this area's development, written for the Montana state's centennial. That was the newspaper back then. During the first years of the development of the town of Beddington, Walter had managed to build his own house, and talked the government into adding his town to the pony express route. He promised quick food, water and a fresh horse to all of the riders when they hit his post. He sent letters to friends in New York and Denver and many other cities to encourage people to come west. He sent articles that were printed in the New York Times and the Chicago Herald newspapers. Walter traded with the Indians of the area and developed amicable relations with them. All were welcome in the town of Beddington.

He figured he was on his way to having one of the largest cities in the west. After a number of years the thrill began to fade for Walter. People were moving to his town by the wagon load. Families came from all over. Walter wanted more. He wanted a wife and a family of his own.

The article from the Montana Centennial described the land and the people going through a great change back then. There were many new settlements that sprung up all over the west during this time. Many people came west before the turn of the Century. They gave up some of the pleasures of their past lives. Some came for the excitement, some came because of persecution, and some were run out of town, from whatever town they were in. Many of the other newly developed towns still had many problems with Indians and gunslingers and some low life folks who were always trying to make a quick buck. There must have been a lot of confusion in those beginning days in the West. This didn't seem to be the case for Beddington. The town had a sheriff and a few deputies, their main job was to help the drifters through town. They didn't allow the gunslingers and lowlifes to hang around too long. Consequently, word spread and more families and fewer troublemakers came to town. People spent more time working on their farms and raising their families and less time pursuing the wild life.

Many families moved to Beddington with the promise of a better life.

Besides the promise of 840 acres for each person and the possibility of gold in the nearby mountain, people from the East began to dream of untold riches of the West. Those dreams also brought many undesirables, however for some reason they didn't stay. Another related article said that Walter had the Sheriff and his Deputies invite each visitor that set foot in Beddington to dinner with Walter himself. Well no one knows what Walter told these folks. Apparently some of the drifters left the very night Walter had them for dinner. There were some reports that Walter shared a secret with them. The way these people disappeared, none of the regular towns folks even wanted to know what the secrets were. The article failed to report any more about what the secret was.

During my internet scanning, I found an old drawing of main street. The street of dirt, wide enough to turn a team of horses and buildings with wooden sidewalks on both sides. Some with a second floor and some without. It looked like a hotel on the corner and a blacksmith shop in the middle of the row of buildings with horses tied up at a front hitching post. The town saloon was unmistakable.

I moved my search to another web site, www.history.com and searched for Beddington, Montana. There were twenty-two sites that listed Beddington. Among the listings was a site that mentioned the Sharpe family.

In March of 1890 the Sharpe family came west and settled in the town of Beddington. That same year, Walter met and married Emily Rebecca Sharpe. That was the same year he started the Beddington manor. He was quoted as telling Emily he would build her the biggest house in the country.

The Beddington Gazette appeared to be a local paper. It was also among the listings on the internet. It spanned from 1883 to 1911. This appeared to be a local paper. Some of the articles included the market rate on cows, pigs, corn and wheat. Other articles were more of a personal nature about Walter and some of the other townsfolk.

The Railroad built a line from Seattle Washington to the connecting East, West route just north of Salt Lake City, Utah. Walter had enough influence to guide the tracks through the town of

Beddington. There was a picture of a man at the new railway station holding a wooden crate labeled FRAGLE-MIRRORS that apparently just arrived from the east. No associated article, just the train depot sign behind him that said BEDDINGTON.

Other research articles said Walter imported workers from all over the United States and built the largest house in this town, probably the biggest house in the state and maybe the country. Meanwhile, Walter got into the Cattle ranching market when cows were selling for two dollars a head, and had a herd of thousands. Between the cattle and the gold, Walter and Emily did very well. Walter never actually worked the gold mines, but paid people well to work it for him. Walter and Emily were, indeed, the richest people in the city and in the state.

When the hills were pretty well mined out, the migration slowed down into Beddington Montana. Some folks left the town to follow the next gold rush. Of course with the safety and calmness of this town, some families continued to come in from the big cities. Walter and Emily stayed, they figured they couldn't leave, it was their town.

I had had enough of my history lesson for today, I had been reading for three hours.

It was getting late and I thought I had a date at 6pm with the little waitress from this morning. I realized I hadn't even gotten her name. I thought, what kind of reporter was I? About 5:30 I walked over to the café to meet up with Miss 'I don't know your name'. I hoped she was still willing to enlighten me on all of the secrets of Beddington Manor. I could not pass on the opportunity to talk to a local, a willing local.

Chapter Nine

I sat down at a table, but could not see my beautiful informant of the evening. An elderly woman came over to the table with a glass of water and a menu.

"Need a minute?" she asked. I looked up and said,

"Hi, ah, well, ah, yeah, is that other girl here?"

"Emma? No, she left hours ago. You must be that reporter fella, yeah, she didn't know your name either. Talked about ya all day though. Wanting to know what you're doing here. She asked everyone that came in today." I told the waitress I might be back in a little while and asked her if she saw Emma to let her know I was looking for her. I walked out onto the sidewalk in front of the restaurant. I saw Emma across the street by the only bar in town, the Fare Inn. She was waving at me, motioning for me to come over. I crossed the street to the bar. I was a little hungry and wanted some dinner. I thought to myself, it was a bar, at least, and maybe we could have a few drinks and a couple of appetizers.

Ha, I laughed to myself, how quaint, drinks before dinner.

"Emma" I said sarcastically, "I'm sorry, I thought we were going to meet at the café." She gave me a quick glance that pierced right through me. I backed off and started with a new attitude, "We really didn't finalize any real plans for this evening, did we."

Emma just said "Didn't get in did ya? Mr. Tom Benson, here harassing the poor folks, are ya? Or is it the OLD FOLKS?" I didn't understand what she was trying to do so I began to get defensive when Emma began to laugh. "A big city writer comes to Twodot, must be some kind of story here. Why are you checking out old Beddington?" I already knew she'd been asking around about me so I just smiled and said, "Can I buy you a drink?"

"Of course you can, if you want the real story of what's going on up there."

I don't know if she really knew anything, but it would be fun trying to find out what she did know.

I was intrigued with Beddington. I never thought of anything sinister or wrong, it was as if the whole town was protecting the old house and all of the residents. I thought I already knew most of the secrets. Old man Beddington had a ton of money, bought everything and everybody and now probably some of his descendents were still doing the same thing. No one wanted any outsider to know about it because everything was going so smooth and everyone was still making money. That's probably why Learchman wouldn't let me talk to the old man today.

I thought the Curator, Learchman must have some hidden agenda. Emma probably knew the story, I figured she would be singing before this night was over.

We entered the Fare Inn, which was dark like most bars and yet clean and absent of the typical fog of smoke. We sat at a corner table, Emma with her back to the wall and positioned to watch the front door.

It must have been too early for the regulars to be here because it was pretty much just the two of us. I ordered a couple of drinks and asked Emma why she didn't meet me in the Café.

"The Café has too many ears. Of course the bar does too, but it's too early for them yet."

I said, "How do you know who I am?"

Emma smiled "Are you kidding? This town knows everything. I asked around, almost *everybody* knows why you're here, who you are, who you were, some of *your* secrets." She paused while the bartender dropped off our drinks. She watched him retreat to the bar. Her eyes returned to mine, "I know your wife died five years ago."

I looked back at her and said, "How could you know that?"

She said, "We have the Internet too, ya know." She went on, "Well Tom, besides knowing all about you, this town here, doesn't cotton to much to strangers, and you see, that's what you are, a stranger." Her tone changed to her best cowboy redneck voice "This town takes care of its own, and we don't want to be written up in some magazine. We don't want to be "of interest" to anybody."

I told her I just wanted to talk to this guy in the Manor. Something about him being the oldest man alive. I told her I already had permission from the granddaughter and that I just needed to have her confirm it.

Emma smiled "She knew you had to have a letter, why didn't she give you one? You know, written permission to see her granddad. She knew you couldn't get in to see old Mr. Johnson without it."

"How did you know it was Mr. Johnson I wanted to see? I never mentioned his name." She smiled and took another sip of her drink.

I pondered and remembered it had been very hard to get a hold of Kate Slybeck all week.

"Why wouldn't she want me to talk to her grandpa?"

"Well," Emma offered "maybe she changed her mind."

I began to defend my position by telling her it should really be no big deal. I thought it might help if I told her that I already knew about Walter Beddington and all of his money. Emma broke in with a surprising offer. "I could get you in to talk to *my* grandmother."

I said, "That would be nice. You would do that?" Emma Just smiled. Of course I thought that as soon as I'm past the Sentry at the front door, I could find Mr. Johnson and have a nice little chat.

"Yes, my grandmother has quite a story. Think you'd like to do a story on *my* Grandmother?"

All of a sudden she became very supportive. She went on. "She used to know Bill Cody, you know Wild Bill Cody? She used to tell us stories all the time of when she was a little girl and they couldn't afford a wagon and horses, so they walked everywhere. Of course back then everything was much closer than it is now, she would say, only five or ten miles. We would all laugh and kid her about walking to school uphill both ways." Emma stopped and confirmed her offer, "Would you like to meet her?"

I said "What about 'a stranger' in town and all of that stuff?" "Oh," she said, "I was just kidding about all of that, and even though there may be some of the others who think that, who cares? You don't care what a few people may think, do ya? And it's not like you're in danger or anything."

My eyebrows raised. She smiled at me and gave a little giggle. I was about to question her motivation, instead I just said "I would love to meet your grandmother."

Emma arranged for me to meet with her grandmother at 10:00 the next morning.

Chapter Ten

True to Emma's word, all I had to do is show up at the Manor the next morning. She had already left word for Mr. Learchman that he was to let me in and escort me to an interview room.

I wondered how many of the residents had been interviewed by the media and if the mystery of their longevity had drawn many other reporters. I figured they converted some small office into an unobtrusive interview room.

As Mr. Learchman was leading me down the hall, I took in the grandeur of the inside of this building. It had hand-carved pillars and portraits of people all over the walls. All of the portraits were of young people, some were people at play and some were informal portraits. Down the hallway was another staircase that led up to the next floor, a sweeping grand staircase, like the kind you see in grand old mansions. I must have been lost in the beauty of the place when I heard Mr. Learchman call my name, "Benson, Benson, this is the room, wait here."

I entered the room, figuring it to be a small room with a table and a few chairs. Instead it was like a giant Library. Hundreds of leather-bound books lined the built in shelves. Old wooden file cabinets ran along the walls. A row of computers sat on a long antique table in the middle of the room. All of the computers were turned on with the screensavers dancing across the screens. I looked at some of the book titles, which included classics by all of the great writers in one section. I then noticed the books organized in like subjects. One section for mysteries, another for self-help, Psychology and Sociology lumped together, and Biographies in the largest section. I looked at the books for a few minutes and moved back over to the line-up of computers. I was just about to touch a key when the door opened again and in walked an elderly woman, white hair, wearing a blue flowered dress. She came in un-assisted, took a look at me and said, "Are you Mr. Benson?" I walked toward her and assured her I was. I showed my credentials and a few magazines I had removed from my briefcase.

"I'm Clara Brand." She said as she extended her hand to shake mine. I shook her hand and we sat down at the computer table across from each other.

"Ya know, I used to be a flapper, you know, a dancing girl" she told me. Emma had told me Clara was born in Eighteen Ninety Seven. If that was true, that would make Clara one hundred and five years old. Just looking at her, I would've guessed not a day over Seventy.

"You granddaughter told me you were born, like a hundred years ago. Is that true?"

As Clara began her story, she said "Eighteen Ninety Seven."

She stopped, glanced over to the computer screen in front of her, looked back to me and said, "I stopped counting, about 87 or 88. I never expected to live this long, so I figured, why count?" She was not shy, but then again she seemed a little uneasy at my presence. She had a nervous laugh and made a little chuckle after each sentence. I told her that it was nice that she used to be a flapper but was thinking, yep she's lost it. She's still living in the Roaring Twenties.

I asked "And when was that, exactly?"

She said "It was 1921. I was only 24. Seemed pretty old then, at least to the other girls" she chuckled.

I had not really planned to interview Clara and was somewhat unprepared. I had planned on escaping straight away to locate Mr. Johnson, but Clara had a story and she seemed willing to share it. I asked if I could use the recorder so I wouldn't miss a single word of her story and told her I didn't want to get any part of her story incorrect, if we *did* publish her story. She was agreeable and then asked, "How much do you pay?"

"Excuse me?" A little shocked I stammered "Pay?"

She laughed that nervous laugh and said, "Granddaughter could use the money."

A knock at the door produced Emma. She stood at the door. She was a radiant beauty, something that I had not noticed last night at the Fare Inn or at the café. She said "hi" and walked over to her grandmother and gave her a kiss on the cheek, whispered something in her ear, and they both had a chuckle. I presumed it was at my expense because they both took a quick glance at me and chuckled again. Emma sat down and asked if I had been here very long. I said I had not and she proceeded to interview me about the questions she thought I should ask.

Emma and her Grandmother asked me all kinds of questions as to why a magazine would be interested in old people anyway, how many other old people had I interviewed and so on.

Clara told me how she grew up in Chicago and moved out west back in the 40's, first to Denver, then to Los Angeles, back to the Dakotas and finally to Montana.

The one thing that makes this job so easy is that people like to talk about themselves. You don't have to ask too many questions and most people like to talk about the subject they know best, Clara was no exception.

I tried to move the conversation a few times to Johnny Johnson. She said she knew him, all right, and moved the conversation back to the time she got to ride on a brand new motorcycle. I asked what kind of food they had there at Beddington. She said they had a special cook who prepared something different for each resident. She said they always ate in their rooms and then after dinner they might get together and talk on the porch or watch the sun go down or visit the library and read or use the computers. I couldn't help but be surprised by the fact that these elderly folks had joined the computer age.

I asked, "You all use the computers?"

"Oh yes, I think everyone here uses them. Oh, of course some of us use them more than others, but I think everyone uses them sometimes."

"And what do they use them for?"

Clara looked at me with a surprised look on her face. "Well, Mr. Benson, you can do all kinds of things with the computer. You can read books, you can read newspapers, you can do research, we can even read *your* magazine on the computer. Did you know your magazine is on there?" She didn't give me a chance to respond. "And of course to communicate with others. Others on the outside."

I said, "Oh yes, of course, e-mail." She just smiled, glanced over to Emma, winked and then back to me.

Whenever Clara mentioned another resident, I pushed other types of questions, like when she mentioned that Mona told her Mr. Joseph really missed his family.

I would ask questions like, "How long have you known Mona?

How long has Mr. Joseph been here?" But Clara wouldn't engage too much about the other residents. She would say she had known Mona for 50 years or Mr. Joseph hadn't seen his kids for 30 or 40 years.

"You know, when I was born, people didn't live this long, no not at all. When my kids sent me here, they thought I was about ready to die," She said.

I asked, "When was that?"

"That was back in 1952, when I was only 55. Can you imagine 55? Would you put your folks in a home when they turned 55, Mr. Benson? It was Mr. Benson, wasn't it? Well that was 50 years ago. Now all of my children are gone. I only have my grandchildren." She said that with a smile to Emma. "I love my Emma."

Emma took her hand. "Grandma, would you like to take a break for a while?"

Clara nodded. "Come back tomorrow." Of course it wasn't even noon yet. However, at that very moment Clara decided the interview was over. She pushed her chair back and asked Emma to walk her to her room. I offered to come along and she agreed, so we all left the interview room. I glanced back at the computer that Clara was sitting in front of as we had been talking. It had a full page of type. Clara did no typing while we were talking, so I was naturally curious as to what was on the computer. Once we were in the hallway, I said, "Oh! I left one of my magazines on the table and I needed to get it."

Clara stopped and Emma said, "We'll wait right here."

I went back into the room directly to the computer screen. Everything Clara had just said was on the screen. At first I thought the computer could have the 'talk and type' program loaded on it. I would've blown it off, except I began to notice that the only words that were on the screen were Clara's. No words from Emma or myself. I might even explain this away with the thought that maybe it was just set to Clara's voice. Then I noticed at the bottom of the screen, after "I love my Emma" and "Come back tomorrow," and in all capital letters it said,

ENOUGH FOR TODAY. YOU ARE TELLING TOO MUCH!

As I was looking at the screen, another line was typed.

HELLO TOM BENSON.

I looked around the room to be sure I was the only one there. I saw no one else. I looked again at the monitor. It was blank. I double checked it and hit the

'Enter' key. Nothing happened. I began to think this was some kind of joke. I again looked around the room. Jack must have something to do with this. I wanted to stay right here and check this further, but knew I was expected. I gathered my magazine and hurried back to where the ladies were waiting for me in the hall. I asked Emma, "Have you ever used the computers here?"

"No," she replied and directed her attention back to Clara. Took her arm and we proceeded to the back side of the stairs.

Chapter Eleven

We took the lift to the second floor and on to Clara's room. The upstairs hallway looked like a ballroom, with doors on both sides, some opened and some closed.

I asked, "Are these the residents rooms?"

Clara was quick to point out, "Oh yes, that one is Mona's and that one is Miss Emily's. Jean Kearns is next to me and Laurie Locke is next to her.

"Laurie Locke, the Laurie Locke?" I said. "The actress?"

Clara laughed a little, and said, "Uh huh, the actress."

"Wow, I thought…I mean, don't take this wrong but I thought she was dead." The flashback in my head saw the headlines. "Laurie Locke Dead at 99". "Laurie Locke passes in her sleep". Pictures of her at 30 and at 90 posted next to the headlines.

Clara looked up at me and said "No no, not at all. You know some of these people announced their death just so people would leave 'em alone. Most are just like me, we all love life too much to give up." She made her familiar little laugh. "I could introduce you to some of the other residents."

I was beside myself and blurted "YES!" I regained control of myself and tried to say calmly, "Or, ah, that would be great. Could we include some of the men too?

Emma said, "I can introduce you to Mr. Johnson right now if you wish."

"I would love that" I said. Emma finished walking Clara to her room, and then came over to me and sort of whispered in my ear, "About that pay thing, we'll talk about it later."

I nodded with a smile on my face, thinking she wouldn't remember. They entered Clara's room, I waited in the hallway.

From the doorway I saw Emma put her in her easy chair and give her a quick kiss on the cheek. She said "I'll be right back Grammy, I'm going to see if we can find Mr. Johnson."

When Emma joined me, she could see the excitement on my face. I was like a schoolboy, breaking the rules. Emma said, "I hope we can find him, and I hope no one catches us." I told Emma we'd be okay so long as Mr. Johnson was okay with it.

Emma said all the women were on the second floor and all of the men were on the first floor, so we had to go back downstairs. We returned to the first floor and toward the back of the building. There was John J. Johnson in rather small letter on the front door. The door was closed so Emma knocked. A man came to the door and asked, "Are you from that magazine?"

Emma said "He is, and I'm Emma Sorensen. My grandmother is Clara Brand."

"Oh I know Clara and I know you too Emma. So you're from the Magazine?" he said as he looked back at me.

I said "Yea, I mean, yes I am. Are you John J. Johnson?"

He stepped out into the hallway, looked at the name on the door and said, with a smile "Yes I am!" He winked at Emma, almost flirting and then to me, "Sure, I'm Johnson, I've heard all about you."

I asked, "How could you have heard about me?

Emma took his arm as we were walking back into his room, looked over her shoulder and said, "I told you this town knows all about you Tom."

I followed them into Mr. Johnson's room. It was spacious. It was like a full-sized house. The living room was bigger than my hotel room and decorated with an unusual and yet eye catching décor. Framed photographs covered one complete wall in the living room, almost from floor to ceiling with photos of young and old alike. Some very old looking medical utensils were displayed in a walled unit covered in glass. A hat rack stood just inside the front door, with hats that appeared to span every era. I could see the kitchen to the right. A hallway led to the back part of the apartment, where I assumed the bedroom and bath were.

"Nice place here. So you like it?" I was still looking around when he caught my eye. He didn't say anything for a minute, but was just looking at me. Emma was sitting next to him and they were both just staring at me as I was rambling on about his nice living quarters.

He smiled at me and asked "Can I get you a drink? How about you Emma?"

"Sure, I could use some coffee, if you still have some" she said.

Mr. Johnson headed for the kitchen, very spry and moving rather quickly. Not like a man 122 years old. I was expecting an old man in a wheelchair or at least small and frail. This man appeared to be healthy and young. I mean he didn't look 40 or 50, but he was not even close to looking like he was anywhere near 122 either.

He looked to be around 75 or so with his gray hair and his quirky sense of humor. I didn't want to rush into the interview, but I did want the information. "Yes sir, this is a very nice place," I started, "How long have you lived here, Mr. Johnson?"

He offered me a cup of coffee when he brought Emma her cup. He said "My granddaughter called and said you were going to come and talk to me about being old. What do you want to know? You know, we don't get as many visitors as we used to. I have been here since Nineteen Fifty, and what year is it now?" He looked over at Emma and gave her a little wink.

I said "Two Thousand Two." Then I notice him chuckling with Emma. A little embarrassed I asked, "Would you mind if I used a recorder?

He looked again at Emma and then back to me. "Why, can't you just remember stuff?"

I glanced up to see him wink at Emma again and she had a little smile on her face. I continued to set up the recorder, "This way I'll get it all correct and won't miss any of the details, okay?"

Mr. Johnson said he didn't mind if I used a recorder, so I turned it on and he began to reminisce. "Well I'll tell ya, I've seen it all. I never thought I'd live this long. You know, when I was young, I mean really young, we didn't have all the things like you all have today. My folks didn't have a car, we grew up without electricity, can you believe it? And what about indoor plumbing? We take so many things for granted today. I remember when my parents took us to a show house. The show was a live performance. Then the movies were made, you're probably too young to remember the silent movies. Used to be a guy there playing the piano during the movie. Anyway then the talkies came to the theater and then larger screens and cine-rama, panavision and surround sound. Hell, finally now we are seeing movies in 3D again, so it appears that we are seeing a live performance, just like the good old days, kind of funny huh?"

Mr. Johnson continued, "Do you know why the price of most things you buy, even today always end in 99 cents? Well, a long time ago that wasn't the case, it used to be all monetary trade was done in even dollars. A man, I think his name was Adolph Ochs, bought a printing press and decided to make a newspaper. Well when sales didn't take off, he couldn't believe that people didn't want to know what was going on in their own back yard. So he started looking around and found out the people that were buying his newspaper had to break a dollar to buy a one-cent paper. This Ochs guy went around to many of the local businesses and convinced them to charge 99 cents or $1.99 or $2.99 or whatever so the people would still have a penny left over so they could buy a paper. In return, he provided a newspaper for free for those businesses that participated. Pretty shrewd considering the business put an extra penny in hundreds of pockets every day, and the newspaper only provided one paper for each business. Obviously sales for the newspaper soared. Consequently the New York Times was born."

Mr. Johnson stopped. "Can I offer you some lunch, Mr. Benson? Emma?"

Emma said she had to get back and check on her grandma.

I asked if I could call her this evening, and she said "I'd like that." She excused herself and Mr. Johnson walked her to his front door.

"Say hi to Clara for me," he said. Emma assured him that she would and walked down the hall and disappeared up the stairs.

Mr. Johnson walked back to the kitchen, opened the fridge and took out a couple of apples. He began to cut them up, I followed him and sat on the barstool on the other side of the counter. With my trusty recorder in hand I asked, "Mr. Johnson, where were you born?"

He continued to cut up the apples precisely into eight wedges and began to cut out the core of each section. He stopped and looked up and said "You can call me John if you'd like."

I smiled and said "Okay, John, where were you born?"

"Why, New York City," he said proudly. "Do you want my whole life story?" He laughed a little, "Not only have I seen everything, I've done everything as well. Did you want to hear about all of the things I've done? Did you want to know about my kids? Or how about my grand children? Do you want to know about my first train ride? Want to know what we do here? How about the Great Depression? I was here for that ya know. Do you want to know about the

Wars, you know the World Wars? Some of you youngsters think between the World Wars and Viet Nam, that those were the only wars there were. Hell, I can remember the Boer War in South Africa and the fighting in the Philippines between the American armed forces and Philippine rebels, seeking independence from the United States back in 1900.

"I can remember the time I met Andrew Carnegie. You know he was good friends with Rockefeller." He went on, "Yes, the turn of the century was quite a time for America. I was just 20 years old, but I remember it like it was just yesterday. You know, some of my children were born at home. That was pretty hard on Lenora. Once we moved here, the hospital was a priority. All of my children were born in the hospital, once the hospital was built. Fourteen in all. Almost unheard of today. How many children do you have, Mr. Benson?" He took a bite of his prepared apple and handed me a plate with the other apple cut and prepared as if we were in a restaurant.

I said "Three, two boys and a girl. When did you move to Denver, John?"

He said "That's nice, most of my children only had one or two kids of their own. They don't know what they missed by not having a big family. We used to have such good times." He was staring into the air for just a minute, he never answered about moving to Denver. I didn't disturb him because I could tell he was just thinking about

his family and his past. It seemed that he had quite a past to remember.

I crunched another apple wedge and it sort of brought him back.

I asked him "What *do* you do here, John?"

"Oh" he said, "We're always busy here. We're quite a social bunch, people coming and going all the time. There are about 50 residents here most of the time, and always something to do. We still get out into the town pretty often. We have a garden, we grow our own vegetables, ya know."

I smiled and asked in sort of a clown voice "And what do you owe your longevity to, Mr. Johnson?" I pretended to have a microphone in my hand and pushed my hand toward him. He played along and took the pretend microphone from my hand saying, "I owe my long life to vegetables from my own garden and waking up every morning." We both chuckled.

Right then a knock came at the door. It was the house Cook, with John's lunch on a cart.

John said, "Oh good, our lunch is here."

I said, "*Our* lunch?"

John said, "I took the liberty, hope you don't mind. You will like this, trust me."

I was surprised because I had not seen John use the telephone or notify anyone of my presence. I didn't know when he ordered lunch for two. Perplexed, I excused myself to the restroom so I could wash up. John directed me down the hall to the first door on the left. I wanted a chance to take a look around at some of the apartment that I hadn't seen yet. Once in the bathroom, I saw that, in place of the mirror over the sink, there was a picture of John. I thought, wow, talk about vanity. I guess it never ends. Even at 122 he still wants to look young. I thought I may have been taking too long and didn't want Mr. Johnson to get the idea I was snooping around, so I washed up and hurried back to the kitchen.

John was setting out a salad with cups holding four different dressings. He took the cover off of a hot plate of noodles smothered in a béarnaise sauce and a side plate held a small slice of New York Cheesecake for dessert. Each plate garnished a small bread roll as well. John covered the noodles up again, and said "Salad?"

I said, "This is very nice of you, I would love a salad. "While we were eating, John continued to talk about New York and coming to Denver back in the 30's, during the Great Depression.

"Came out to Denver on a train," he said. "I used to be a Doctor." The package I had received from the Hall of records was still fresh in my mind, and all of the diplomas flashed back into my head. He went on about how he met his wife and how they got free land, "All we had to do was build a house on it. Lenora had a baby almost every year for the next 15 years. Good thing I was a doctor. Of course we didn't make the kind of money the doctors make today. We did okay, even with 14 kids. And I played the stock market. After the Depression, that is."

He said that he always knew the Stock Market would come back, so John took part of his pay each week and invested in Stock. He knew things, things that today would be called insider's secrets. He knew IBM already had a little computer that was smaller than a car and that it could do more than the first and second models were doing. So he invested in IBM back in Nineteen Forty. Then it was called Fortron.

He knew about General Motors and Ford and some other big names, so he put a little money away each week and invested. Later those companies and a few others would prove to provide John and Lenora all the pleasures they never knew as youngsters.

I asked, "John, how did you know about companies like IBM and General Motors?"

"Friends." He said. "Really good friends." He just stared at me. As I began to press, he raised his hand as if he was stopping traffic. I concluded he didn't want to expound.

I asked about some of the other residents, Mona and Mr. Joseph and Jean Kearns, "How old are those people?"

He said he was not too sure how old they were, but he figured around a hundred.

I asked "And Miss Clara, how old is she?"

He again just looked off for a minute. "How 'bout the main course? Smells pretty good, huh?" He put his salad plate back on the tray and brought over the noodle dish. "Dig in, won't stay hot forever, ya know?"

The changing of the cassette tape was the only measure of time for the rest of the afternoon. John talked about everything from the stock market to how he felt about space travel. He shared his thoughts of some of the other residents and William Learchman. He thought Learchman was more than the curator for the Manor. He thought he was the guard. He didn't say the guard of what.

I thought it was just too strange that there were this many people over 100 all in the same place. I decided that I needed to get some verification. I already had some information on the old man, but I needed something on some of the other residents. I again excused myself to the bathroom and while there, I found John's hairbrush. I took some of his hair from the brush and just shoved it into my pocket. I thought it might be a little obvious me asking for a sealed plastic bag. I figured I could have the hair carbon dated. It didn't have to be pure, this wasn't for a DNA or anything like that. I just wanted to know how old his hair was.

We finished our lunch, and dessert and talked for a while longer. John had a healthy appetite and looked extremely fit for a man of his age, whatever that really was. I asked if I may see him again the following day. He agreed and said he would look forward to it.

I realized it had been about five hours since I'd seen Emma or Clara and I thought I should say goodbye before just walking out. It was about 4:00 in the afternoon and many of the residents were in the hallway now, but no sign of Clara. I went upstairs to her room and poked my head in, calling her name, but no answer. I noticed her living quarters were not quite as large as Mr. Johnson's. It was more like a hotel room, a very large hotel room, but the bedroom and living room were connected and a smaller kitchen sat off to the side. I noticed her dresser across the room and thought of Mr. Johnson's hair in my pocket. I thought, well, I could get a little of hers and have them both done at the same time. Background information, I told myself. I entered her room and went directly to her bureau to retrieve some hair from her brush. I noticed the top of the bureau was turned all the way over so you couldn't see the mirror. When I looked behind it, the other side was empty as well.

The thought crossed my mind, I wonder if they take all the glass away from these old folks? I collected my hair sample and stuffed it into the opposite pocket of my jacket. As I turned around to leave, Miss Clara Brand was standing in her doorway looking right at me.

"Oh, hi Clara, I just came up to say goodbye."

She entered the room and said, "I'm telling." She sank into her easy chair and did not utter another word.

I said, "Well okay then, I guess I'll talk to you tomorrow? We have a date, don't forget. Okay?" She didn't look at me, she was just looking at the top of the bureau where the mirror was supposed to be.

I left the room feeling a bit low and I knew if Clara raised a stink, Mr. Learchman wouldn't even consider letting me back in. I knew for now, I'd better leave. Of course after the nice lunch I had with Mr. Johnson, I needed to use the facilities one more time. I didn't want to knock on one of the resident's doors and I did notice there were bathrooms in the hallway. As I entered the rest room, I again took notice to the size of the room. The room was very large and had tile on the walls as well as the floor and matching tile on the ceiling. There were six private stalls and eight wash basins. A full mirror spanned all of the wash basins and towel dispensers hung on both ends of the room. The room had large frosted windows at the other end so the room could be flooded with sunlight. However that would be morning light and this time of day the lights were turned on. I noticed the lighting was very poor. Of the six overhead lights, only four had bulbs and they were very dim. It seemed too early for the sun to be setting, but this was a dark room, not like the rest of the Manor. Although everything was very clean, it looked like this room didn't get much use. Then again, why should it. I assumed each resident had his or her own bathroom in their quarters.

As I was washing my hands, I glanced into the mirror and noticed someone else had entered the room and was already in one of the stalls. I glanced back at myself and in my reflection I noticed my left eye was a little slow to straighten out. I shook my head and just figured it was because I was looking and the guy's feet in the stall and looking at my self through the mirror at the same time. I turned off the faucets and headed to the paper towel rack to dry my hands. As I was walking toward the door, I said out loud, "Well have a nice day."

There was no answer. I stopped and said it again, "Have a nice day." Still no response. I walked back toward the stall. I said, "Are you okay?" All was quiet. I began to knock on the stall door and it swung open. I said "Are you ..." and stopped in mid-sentence. No one was there. I looked in the next stall; no one there, either.

I thought, how could that old man get in and out of here without me hearing or seeing him? Did he even wash his hands? He couldn't have. I checked the sinks one more time, mine was the only one that was wet. I looked up at myself in the mirror and out of the corner of my eye I saw one of the stall doors close. I turned around to see it and again, nothing appeared to have moved. I looked again in the mirror and saw nothing. I turned around and walked slowly over to the stall. I pushed the stall door open slowly, my heart racing, I thought to myself, I hope no one is here, this is going to be so embarrassing. The door opened on an empty stall. Okay I thought, they needed to get better lighting in here. My eyes are playing tricks on me. I walked back out of the stall and again was heading for the door, glanced into the mirror one more time and just saw the side of my head. When I stopped and blinked, I was just looking at myself like normal.

I looked away and back several times, and each time everything appeared normal. I left the bathroom, left the Manor and walked back to my safe hotel room. I had to admit to myself that all was not normal. I was looking forward to seeing Emma in a few hours. She would have the answers. She knew what was going on.

Chapter Twelve

I took refuge from the world in this hotel room. This was a place I had not even known just two days ago, now somehow I felt comfortable and normal here. I sat at my hotel room desk with my computer and my trusted tape recorder. I was about to start to type the beginning of my story. While the tape was rewinding, I looked in the dresser mirror, puffed out my chest and sucked in my gut just a bit and said to myself "I did good today."

As I thought back to my day, I realized that the building, Beddington Manor, itself was an important part of my story. I should have taken more notice of the exterior of the building because it seemed the dimensions on the outside didn't match the inside. I had already been to Beddington Manor twice and each time I wanted to check that out. Yet each time I left the Manor I left in a state of confusion and bewilderment, the first time because of the odd curator, Mr. Learchman, and the second time, well, I was still trying to understand what happened in that bathroom.

The tape had stopped rewinding and was ready to be flipped and played. I thought I could get a few pages done before I needed to get ready for dinner with Emma. I was about to call Emma to firm up the plans for dinner when a knock came at the door.

I opened the door to find Emma standing there, looking beautiful. "Well, can I come in?" she said in a somewhat seductive tone. Or maybe I just thought it was seductive.

"Of course you can. Please, come in. How did you know where I was? Oh yeah, everybody knows where I am. You know, if everybody *does* know that I'm here and what I'm doing, how do they, all the ones that know, feel about it? And how do they feel about Beddington? Does everyone in this town have someone up there?"

Emma had walked in and was standing by the window. She said "Whoa, you ask a lot of questions. Do people usually answer all of your questions?

"Usually," I said. I could tell she was agitated.

Did you enjoy yourself today Tom?" she sparred.

"Well, yes I did" I said. "It was a pretty nice day. You know, I never knew what types of experiences, historical information and stories these old… I mean these senior citizens could share, all of the things *they* have experienced. I have to admit, I have undervalued these folks. What is it that keeps them so young?"

"I guess you did have a good time today" Emma said, "You certainly seem pretty excited about something. Did you ask any of *them* what keeps them so young?

"Well I..." she cut me off, and said, "Do you really think they are as old as they say they are? I mean, you thought they were lying about that earlier today. Right? Clara said something about you taking her hairbrush? Did you take her hairbrush?"

I knew from Clara's reaction to me in her room that I would probably be in trouble with Emma. "No, of course not." I said "I did take some of her hair from her hairbrush, though. I thought I could send it over to Denver and have it carbon-dated to verify her age. I did the same with Mr. Johnson's hair from his hairbrush. Is that a problem? Did you know Mr. Johnson says he is 122 years old? Do you think he looks that old?

Emma just shook her head. "Tom, were you in Clara's room without her permission? Did you just go into her room with no one there and start snooping around? Do you know how lucky you are to even be in Beddington? You shouldn't try to piss everybody off the first day you're there."

"Oh Emma, I'm so sorry. I never intended to offend anyone.

I am very grateful to be allowed into Beddington. Why is there so much security there anyway? Learchman is like a sentry. Each person is cleared before they can even talk to a resident? What's that about?" I figured Emma knew much more than she was letting on.

She ignored my last questions and went back to the easy one. "No, I didn't know how old Johnson was," she said.

"Did you know that almost everyone in that home is over one hundred?" I continued, "Yes, I was in Clara's room, I knocked on the door and it just sort of swung open. I called for her but no one answered. I was concerned about her welfare, and the truth of the matter is I was curious about her as well, and if I *am* going to do a story on her, I need as much information, verified information as I can get. How many years has Clara been in Beddington? How long have you been going there to see her?

"I've been going to Beddington Manor since I was just a little girl. We used to go there and play while my parents visited Clara. So Clara has been there for a very long time, most of my life. What's your point, Tom?"

I thought about it for a minute. "This is a bigger story than just Mr. Johnson being the oldest man in America," I said. "There is something else going on here. Don't you think?"

"Yes, I knew that almost everyone there is over a hundred years old. What gives?" Apparently Emma thought it was normal for all of these people to be over 100.

I said, "As far as I know there has never been a concentration of this many people this old in any retirement home, old folks home, whatever you want to call it. I can smell something going on."

"Tom, there are people here who probably don't want a story of Beddington written."

"Why, what are they hiding?"

Emma looked away and said, "They're not hiding anything, they just want to grow old gracefully. Think about it, Tom, if it were your parents or grandparents, would you like someone doing an exposé on them?"

She changed the subject and said, "Where are you taking me to dinner?" The room fell quiet for a few minutes. I thought I would give it a rest for a little while, I could tell she was getting upset, and I had the rest of night to spend with her.

I said "I was thinking of this little place in Paradise. I noticed it when I was driving up here. I hope they're open. It's called Diamond Lil's.

Emma said she knew the place and could show me a smoother way to get there instead of the dirt road that connected the two towns.

I said, "I would rather go a hundred miles out of our way before I did the dirt washboard again." I figured that once I had her in the car I would put on my best interview. I needed some answers and I knew Emma knew more than I had heard so far.

We headed toward Paradise on a paved 60-mile detour. Switchback roads, lined with pines. The Sun was just setting as we went over the crest of the hill. The Sunset was beautiful, Emma looked over to me, caught my eye and smiled in contentment. I told Emma about the time I had spent with Mr. Johnson and some of the items we had talked about. I said, "Every time I talked about his age, he sort of changed the subject. However, he began to act his age and drift off. He began rambling into another conversation and never got back to his age, but when I asked Clara's about her age, it seemed she was proud that she was 105. You know, if there is some secret, like Kate Slybeck had hinted about, these people could bottle it. Make a million bucks."

Emma listened to me go on and on, and then she said, "Do the people up there look like they need more money? It seems like every need they have is being fulfilled. How much more money do you think they should have? If all of their needs and wants are taken care of, you know, I don't think they are interested in any more money. Most of them have outlived their children. Most people in the world don't even know they exist."

She continued, "You asked me earlier if everyone in town had someone in Beddington. I'd say everyone in Beddington has someone in Twodot. My great grandparents came here during the gold rush, my grandparents lived here their whole lives. My parents lived here most of their lives, and I was born here as well. I left for a little while. I came back ten years ago and I hope I never leave again. I hope some day I will be able to live in Beddington. My parents moved away, wanted to go to the big city. They went to Los Angeles in 1980. Three weeks after they arrived, they were killed for my dad's wallet and my mom's purse. Some gang thing, the kids were never caught. I guess my folks never thought about the fact that they were almost the only people on the street. Here you can walk anywhere you want, any time you want. And do you know the worst thing that can happen to you? The worst thing that can happen to you in Twodot, someone might talk about you. That's it. Someone might talk about you. Well, you know, I wish someone was talking about my parents right now."

I put my arm around Emma and tried to comfort her a little. "You know," she said, "Some people in town don't want this story out. They like life in Twodot just the way it is".

I wasn't surprised at her statement and sensed the selfishness of the entire town. I asked, "Well Emma, if the people of Beddington Manor have found the fountain of youth, don't they have a moral obligation to share it?"

Emma pulled away from my arm and said, "Do you want to open this Pandora's box? This fountain of youth may be just that. And besides, if the residents of the Manor wanted to share the fountain of youth with the world, don't you *think* they would have done it before now?"

It was dark by the time we pulled into Paradise. Most of the businesses along Main street were shut down for the night. There were three other cars in the parking lot. We walked into Diamond Lil's and were immediately seated. Diamond Lil's was the closest thing to a real restaurant within miles of Twodot, with linens and cloth napkins on the table. We had a wonderful dinner and talked about little things for a while. Emma didn't want to talk about Beddington and the seniors. We had some wine with dinner and started feeling pretty good. I knew she had information that she was holding onto. It was like a secret and she was not about to tell.

I directed the conversation back to her and let her talk about herself and her parents and pretty much about her life. She wanted to know little about me, but mostly wanted to talk about herself. However, each conversation and topic always returned us to the Manor. How she was angry with her parents for going to California. How they could have both been in

Beddington right now. How all of her brothers and sisters had left town and she is the only one to take care of Clara. How she had been going to see Clara for over 30 years.

I asked, "Have you ever been married?"

"Yes, that's when I left. You know being a waitress, you get to meet a lot of people. Well, I met this construction guy who was working on the Manor and he talked a good story and we became good friends. One thing lead to another and I wound up married to the guy and living in Denver. I got another waitress job and he worked the local area in construction. We found that we really didn't know each other very well. Well really, not at all. You know, the classic story, everything that attracted me to him I grew to hate. The same for him, I guess. He thought because I worked in a restaurant, I liked to cook. I told him I worked in a restaurant because I hated to cook. With him being a laborer, I figured he would be happy if I just brought dinner home each night. So that bugged him. He had a Harley and he was always out riding with his friends.

That bugged me, and it was just one thing after another. I missed Twodot and I wanted to get back home and he wanted me out of his. So, it was divorce city and I came running back home. Of course both of my parents were gone and my brothers and sister were spread out all over the country, but this was home. And I had Clara. I guess I needed Clara more that she needed me. So here I am, married, divorced and still waitressing in Twodot."

"Do you ever talk to him?"

"My ex? No we both figured it was a mistake. I haven't seen him since I left Denver."

We both shared stories from our past. It was the game of twenty questions in a relaxed setting. I continued to guide the conversation back to the Manor. I told her about my bathroom experience. I told her about the guy in the stall, and how he wouldn't talk, and when I opened the stall door, he was gone. I asked her if she had heard about anything like that before, or if it had ever happened to her. She said she heard about a reporter who went to the Manor to interview someone years ago and no one ever saw him again. Then she laughed. I laughed along with her, while trying to talk the hair on the back of my neck into relaxing.

Emma went on, "You know, just when you think something is weird up there and someone finds out that all of the people in the old folks home are really *old*, and you wonder why they never die, well someone does. Mary Jo Whitehead died about a year ago. She was 102.

I asked, "Was it a suspicious death?"

Emma looked up and said, "It's never suspicious when you're 102.

"So how could you see a guy go into a stall and he, what, just disappeared?" Emma ordered another glass of wine. "And you say you saw him twice and he disappeared twice? Maybe your eyes were just playing tricks on you? Maybe one of those 100-year-old guys were so quick you didn't see him leave. And why would any of them use the main rest room, anyway? Each one of them has a bathroom in their apartment. I have been to the Manor a million times and I have yet to see one of those women in the main bathroom." The wheels in Emma's head were turning,

"You know, I was with Clara one time and she said she would rather go up to her room before she ever thought about using the public facilities."

Right then the waiter came over and asked if we would like dessert, I looked at Emma, she just held up her empty glass and said, "I would rather drink my dessert, if you don't mind." We both ordered one more glass of wine and smiled at the way we felt.

On the drive home, I tried to control the conversation. I said I was surprised that Clara and the others were computer users.

"Uh huh." She said, not offering much. She sat with her head against the headrest and her eyes straight forward.

I stopped at Emma's house and walked her up to the front door. I gave her a little kiss good night, she kissed me back, and invited me in for another drink. I accepted and entered her house. It was a cute little bungalow-style home. She glanced at me as I looked around and asked if I'd like the grand tour. I nodded, and she took me from room to room. It turned out to be a two-bedroom, two-bath masterpiece that was built in the early 1900's. She had family pictures all over the walls and a piano in the living room. Her second bedroom had been turned into an office and contained a computer desk with all of the latest computer equipment intact. We wandered back into the kitchen, where she opened a bottle of wine and poured us both a drink.

She started, "You know, even if there is more going on up at Beddington, I mean really, so what? You are here to do a story on some of the old folks, right? I mean, Johnny Johnson is suppose to be 122 and Clara, well she's 105 and all. That *is* your purpose, right?" I told her about the newspaper article about Mr. Johnson in Denver.

"His daughter called the newspaper and just wanted the paper to announce his birthday. The Denver Post put it in their paper. She cut out the article and showed it to her grandpa and, according to her, it was all for a smile from him. Well my boss gets this article and thinks things don't add up. I find this Kate Slybeck and she tells me it was for her father's great-grandfather. Kate tells me that her grandfather is dead, her father is dead, and here is Mr. Johnny J. Johnson, 122 years old who has outlived his own child and at least one of his grandchildren, probably outlived all of 'em. That makes Kate Slybeck Mr. Johnson's great, great-granddaughter."

Emma was pouring another drink as we were talking. We had reclined to the sofa and were getting very comfortable.

"Anyway, my boss sends me here to talk to Mr. Johnson to get the secrets of life. I get here and find Beddington and nearly everyone there's over a hundred."

Emma just smiled and raised her glass to her lips again.

"Here's to Beddington." She said.

She didn't stop me from talking, but didn't seem surprised by my story.

She placed her glass on the coffee table and reached over to kiss me. I, didn't hesitate. In the middle of her kiss, however, she sort of stopped kissing me. I opened my eyes to see her eyes still closed. She was still pushing against me. It took a few more seconds for me to realize she was asleep.

I had either bored her to sleep or the wine finally kicked in, just a little too soon. I picked her up and transported her to her bed. I covered her with the quilt and returned to the living room. I looked again at the pictures of her relatives and marveled at her dedication to Clara. I let myself out and locked the door behind me.

Back at the hotel, I still wanted to hear my taped conversations from earlier today.

I was listening to the tape and started to doze off. I got up and walked around the room while the tape was playing. I was listening for something that Clara said or maybe something slipped out or maybe something she was not saying, or maybe something that Mr. Johnson didn't say. You know, like listening between the lines.

As the tape played, I dozed again and again, and finally shut the machine off and went to bed.

In the middle of the night, I woke up, cursed about all the wine I drank and headed to the bathroom. As I was washing my hands I looked into the mirror. As I stared into it, I could see my reflection turning older and older and older. I put my hand up to the mirror and my hand was that of an old man. I shook my head and squeezed my eyes shut and opened them again.

As I opened them I found myself still in my hotel bed. I jumped out of bed and ran to the bathroom, directly to the mirror. I began to feel my face and looked into the mirror again. The reflection that was directly in front of me just two seconds ago was gone. Out of the corner of my eye I noticed a movement to my right. I turned my head around to see my reflection standing right next to me. We were both doing the same thing and both seemed to be very surprised. I looked back at the mirror and sure enough, my reflection was now there, I quickly turned back to my three-dimensional self and there was nothing there. I again looked into the mirror to see if it had moved or was starring back. My reflection was smiling at me and beginning to laugh. I lifted my hand to my mouth to make sure I was not grinning. I was not. Right then I could hear the alarm clock going off in the other room. Faintly at first and then it got louder and louder. I woke from my bed with a start. I reached over and turned off the alarm and wasn't sure if I had even been out of bed during the night at all.

Chapter Thirteen

Today I figured I could talk again to Mr. Johnson and maybe even to Clara, if she wasn't too mad at me. I still needed to check on Emma and thank her for last night. I wanted to talk about my dream, and so far, Emma was the only one who might understand. I headed for the café to see Emma and, of course, to have breakfast.

"Good morning," I directed to Emma. I didn't see anyone else in the café. "I just wanted to say I had a good time last night. What a great dinner."

"Hi Tom, I had a good time too, what I can remember of it. When I start drinking, I start talking and talking. I'm sure I did that last night. I'm sure I just went on and on, didn't I?" In fact, Emma hardly had a thing to say once we left the restaurant. "Come over here a minute." She acted as if she didn't remember, or maybe didn't want to remember too much of the previous evening. She directed me to a table and went to the kitchen. She returned with a carafe of coffee and poured a cup for me and then herself.

"I had the strangest dream last night," she started, "I dreamt we went to dinner and we were the only young people. All of the waiters were old, and I mean really old.

Everywhere we looked and everywhere we went, we were surrounded by old, old people. I'm sure it has to do with your story, what do you think? I really don't talk about the Manor too much. But maybe because you kept asking all of those questions..." Her voice trailed off as she heard the bell from the cook and went to retrieve an order for another customer. She delivered it to the table and headed back to me in a split second.

She went on to explain, "The Manor is just part of us. It would be like you talking about your car. You know, everyone knows it's dark green, well you certainly don't go telling everyone you have a green car, right?"

I thought I knew what she meant. I recalled *my* experience in front of the mirror in the middle of the night and began to share it with her, we both kind of laughed and I asked "What were we drinking last night?" I didn't tell Emma that I didn't think mine *was* a dream. I was almost positive it was not, but I didn't want Emma to think I was a total nut case. I tried to talk normal, but I was truly shaken and I had hoped Emma had a similar story or could at least say that she had heard of something like this happening to someone else in town.

I sipped on my coffee and said, "I would really like to know more about the Manor. I would like to know how it's possible that anyone could live to be 122 years old and the whole world isn't here to find out why this old guy is still alive. I get here and find the whole place is full of people that are as old or older than the so-called oldest person in the world. According to the World Press, the oldest human is living in South America and is 107.

She could hear the frustration in my voice. What I hoped she couldn't distinguish was the fear in my tone. Emma reached across the table, touched my hand and said, "Would you like me to go with you today? You know, up to Beddington?" I thought it would be nice to have her with me.

Selfishly I said "Yes, that would be wonderful if you could." Emma began to rise to get back to work, I stopped her when I asked "Emma, do you know what is going on up there?"

She shook her head and sat back down, "Whatever is going on is wonderful. My grandmother is still here and I love her very much. Both of my parents are gone, my family is spread all over the country and so she is my only real link to my past. I don't think you understand the impact your story will have. On them, on the whole town, and maybe to every person that reads it. Once you write all about this, things will change, lives will change, and all for what? To sell a few magazines? You're right, Tom, there is something going on up there, something really good. Come with me tonight, and maybe you'll get a little smarter." Her request was more of an order than a plea for accompaniment.

I was being held in awe and yet disbelief. Emma had my attention, "Just tell me what it is, can't you just tell me?"

She wouldn't give in. She just said, "I'll meet you there at eight." With that, she went back to her duties as a waitress and seated the people that had just come in the door. She walked by my table, looked at me and just mouthed the word 'tonight'. She disappeared into the back of the restaurant, I left five bucks on the table to pay for the coffee and headed back to the hotel.

I was typing up some of the conversation that I had with Mr. Johnson, and was building a list of things that were still unclear. I had asked him if I could come back, and of course he was nice enough to invite me back anytime I wanted. I figured I could go back today and clear up some of the questions on my list. Then tonight, I would meet up with Emma and get a little smarter.

After lunch, I headed up to the Manor. As I walked up the steps to the Manor, I noted how many windows were on the side of the building. Maybe I could take a more careful look at the dimensions on the inside also. I walked into the foyer and immediately Learchman met me there. I asked if I might be able to talk to Mr. Johnson. Learchman said he would ring his room. He could have done that yesterday. I thought, why he didn't was anyone's guess.

Mr. Johnson came to the lobby, saying "Hi, Tom Benson" and reached out his hand. Again I could tell from his grip he was still very healthy. He asked if there was anything he could do for me. I told him I still had a few questions, and he invited me back to his house sized apartment. As I was walking down the hall, I did note that the windows were considerably larger from the inside than they appeared to be on the outside.

We arrived in Mr. Johnson's living room and he asked if I would like some coffee. I said "That would be nice," and he proceeded to pour us both a cup.

As we were drinking our coffee, he began, "Are you a little confused? Did I give you too much information yesterday?

You do believe it all. Ha, I knew you'd be back. You know I've talked to a hundred reporters just like you, Tom. I've narrowed all reporters down to three types." I was hanging on his words. Learning something from someone with all this wisdom was unexpected. He went on. "Some of them act like they believe everything I tell them and yet I never see the story, which meant they didn't really believe me or their boss didn't believe them and so they couldn't print it. Some don't believe a thing I say and they never write the story, which is okay, and I can usually tell if my audience is receptive or not. And when I run into one of those people, I really expect very little. And then there are some like you, Mr. Benson, reporters like yourself keep coming back to verify the facts, always wanting more verification. You see, until you believe it yourself, you can't print it. It's one of those things that you can see, but you can't explain.

Some people just think it is in our genes. You heard of the longevity gene? Well you know, we might have it, some scientists came up here a few years ago, wanted to test us. Well, they poked and prodded and took so much body fluid, I'm surprised we all didn't just blow away. Anyway, they did their tests on us and I guess some of us had that old age gene and some of us didn't. So they sort of dropped it or at least dropped us from the test group. They couldn't explain it, either. You see, they couldn't explain how come all of us are so healthy and yet only a few of us had the lucky gene. None of us took it too serious. Oh, we all took the money they paid us for being their guinea pigs and went on being who we were." He put his finger to his head, paused and

then blurted out, "They gave us a thousand dollars, by golly."

"Does anyone die up here" I asked.

"Oh sure people always die, they die here just like they die everywhere else. Up here we just die a little healthier and maybe a little later. You know you only have so much time here on earth. You've heard 'when it's your time, it's your time' haven't you? Well, we all have it."

"Have what?" I asked.

"Time, we all have just so much time and when your time runs out, you die. We all know that, no one likes to think about it too much. You know, we all love life and that is why no one likes to think about death. Here in the Manor, we figured that out. We try to keep ourselves healthy and do the right things, but we all know we will run out of time eventually.

I will let you in on a big secret Tom Benson." I was hanging on his every word. I figured this was it, the old man had figured out the secret to longevity and was about to share it with me.

"We all have the same amount of time on this planet," He began, "Barring any accidents and all of those stupid things you do to shorten your life, we all have the same number of years, months, days and hours to live. If you live to a ripe old age, like some of us, you'll be able to use all of those years, months, days and hours yourself."

I leaned back in the chair, disgusted and said. "That's it? That is the big secret? We all have the same number of years to live? Mr. Johnson, I don't mean to question your theory on the aging process, but how would you explain that almost every single person dies at a different age?" Mr. Johnson looked down at the floor and appeared to feel a little rejected. I quickly smoothed over my obvious doubt and asked, "How many years do we all have?"

Mr. Johnson looked up and smiled. "It's not done that way." He stopped and looked deep into me. I waited for him to finish his thought. He began again after a calculated pause.

"It's done in hours. You see, we all get the same amount.

We all start out with one million hours."

"We all have a million hours?" I repeated. "A million hours of what?"

"A million hours of life." He said this without hesitation.

I didn't know whether to laugh or pull out the recorder. I chose the latter and he went on.

"It's kind of hard to figure because most people don't keep track. You see, you don't have to count your sleeping hours, because you are not using your hours then. So instead of figuring twenty-four hours a day, you should be figuring only about sixteen hours a day. That is, of course, if you get eight hours of sleep each night. But then again, you need to double the bad habit hours." He looked away from me and appeared to think about it for a minute. He was doing some figuring and counting his fingers.

"Basically," he started again, "Because you're using a regular hour and the time you use on your bad habits, well you're hurting your future and killing your hours with all those bad habits. So for instance, if you smoke for, say two hours a day, and you are awake for twelve hours, instead of using up twelve hours of your million, you use fourteen. Get it?"

I was doing the math in my head and looked up at Mr. Johnson. He just smiled. I said, "That still doesn't explain the age variation of people dying. Some people die at thirty and some at, well obviously over one hundred." I pulled my calculator out of my coat pocket.

"Well," he said. "There are many variables. For instance if you are in a car crash, or any accident for that matter, that may end the timeline for you. You are really not guaranteed the million hours, you just get a million. What you do with your hours is up to you. I spent most of my life trying to extend people's hours on earth. And of course there are the mirror people. They also use up your hours."

I was punching numbers into a calculator. I looked up from what I was doing.

"The what?" I stopped punching.

"The mirror people" he replied. "Yes, you share your hours with your reflections as well. Each time you look into the mirror your reflection uses your hours. Consequently, he uses the same number of hours that you use while *you* are looking at the mirror. I'm pretty sure they keep track."

Again, I didn't know if Mr. Johnson was just having fun with me, or if he was the enlightened scholar I had always wanted to interrogate, or maybe his senility was beginning to come through. For the first time in my life, I was not in control of the interview.

"I'm sorry, I am totally lost now. Who's in the mirror?

Sharing hours, with who? I guess I don't get it."

Mr. Johnson came over and sat down across from me in the living room. He said, "I hate explaining this, mostly because no one believes me and they think I've lost my marbles. And then again I love explaining this for the very same reason." He chuckled. "Anyway, here goes. Every time you look into the mirror, the reflection that looks just like you is looking back, right?" I nodded and double-checked the tape player. "What do you think that is? Do you think it's you in the mirror? It couldn't be *you* because *you* are standing on this side of the mirror, right? Maybe a reflection on the glass? You think that's what it is? What you're looking at, Mr. Benson, is another world. There are people living on the other side of the mirror. They survive only because we do.

Have you ever looked into the mirror and not seen your reflection?"

I had a quick flashback to my hotel bathroom, when I looked to the right to see my three-dimensional self. It was only for a second or two, but it was there.

Mr. Johnson continued to talk. "Probably not. You see, each time you look into the mirror, any mirror, your reflection is there. You're not there, just your reflection. I thought people would have figured this out years ago. We used to say how good *we* looked in the mirror, and now we refer to them as *our reflection*, you know, how good your reflection looks. I thought when that started, you would all figure out that the person in the mirror is not really you. It's another person that looks just like you and whose only job in life is to do everything you do while you're standing in front of the window to their world. You see, they've figured out that if they do everything you do in front of the mirror, you won't want to come over to their side of the mirror."

I didn't ask Mr. Johnson why we might want to go their side of the mirror. I figured this was how he saw it and believed it as the truth. "Oh, and they live off of your million hours of life." He concluded.

Chapter Fourteen

I thought I had heard everything, but this was almost comical. It would have been very funny if I wasn't talking to a man who was 122 years old. I could have completely discounted his story had it not been for my freaky hotel mirror experience just the night before, and the fact that he was, well, 122.

"How long have you known about *this*?" I asked.

"About 70 years." He responded.

"How did you learn about this?"

He looked back at me and said "Walter Beddington."

"How many people know about it?"

"Well, everyone here. Maybe some, or all of the family members." He sat back in the sofa, crossed his leg over the other.

I thought for just a minute and asked. "How did Walter figure it out?"

He added, "Well, when Emily moved here from the East and Walter started building this place, the mirrors they brought with them didn't fare so well. Walter sent back east for some new ones, but it took over three years for them to arrive. They came in on the train. The whole town came out. You're too young to remember, but at one time, mirrors were a precious commodity. No one had 'em, they were very fragile and broke very easily. So it was a big event. Most, no, all of the townsfolk hadn't even looked into a mirror for over three years or more. So when the Beddington mirrors came in, they were displayed at the post office for a few days before Walter put them in his new home.

Well, one by one the townsfolk came to look into the mirror, and one by one, each person that looked into the mirror, aged by about three or four years. Now three or four years doesn't sound like very much, but it's said that some of the kids, came out of the post office 4 inches taller than when they went in. And all of the women that looked into the mirror instantly added wrinkles to their faces. The men got a little fatter and everyone was a lot less happy.

When Emily looked into the mirror, she must have gained much more than three or four years of age. For some reason it looked like she gained twenty years that very day. As most people looked into the mirror and began to see themselves change, they quickly looked away. When Emily looked in, she stared and stared at herself growing older. After she figured she wasn't going to stop aging, she broke the mirror. Slammed it down right there in the post office. Then she broke down and began to cry.

Walter had to help her out of the post office and back up to the manor.

Well some of the townsfolk took the state map right off the post office wall and scratched the name Beddington off of the map. As they were all in and around the post office, someone said. 'Well if this isn't Beddington, what is it?'

"Another citizen said. 'Well it sure ain't Paradise.' They all knew that Paradise was just down the road. However on the map, it was never labeled as such. And now that one of the other townsmen had already defaced the map, and scratched out Beddington, the only thing left was two dots on the map to represent the cities, Paradise and Beddington.

Someone looked at the map and blurted. 'Two dots.'

Another said, 'Twodot it is.'

"So the town was renamed by a handful of citizens. Most of the people felt relieved to no longer be in the town of Beddington. The crowd was so worked up, no one even challenged the new town name and that's how Twodot came to be. Well needless to say, there were never any mirrors allowed in Twodot after that incident.

"That was a long time ago. Most of those people that aged so rapidly that day, no longer live in this town. Some left, some died years later and some moved in right here... Walter and Emily went into seclusion for years. They never came out of the Manor. Mr. Learchman took over the business of building the Manor. Construction never stopped. It went on day and night. Mr. Learchman didn't come out too often. We all wondered if the Beddingtons had passed on. Then just like they disappeared, they returned on a Sunday at a Church Social. Emily wore a veil from that day on. She said she was fine, whenever you talked to her. However, you couldn't see her face. Oh, the town hated the Beddingtons for a while. However things change, and people got over their hatred eventually. For years there were no mirrors allowed in the town of Twodot." He paused, settled down and just looked up from the floor.

"What about now?" I asked.

"Well, time heals all wounds," he said. "Mirrors are allowed in town now, like I said, almost all of the folks involved are either dead or gone, or right here. You'd still be pretty hard- pressed to find a mirror in any of the rooms in Beddington Manor, though. Old man Beddington felt so bad about the whole thing, he just kept adding on to the Manor, he and Learchman. He let most of the workers go and then it was just the two of them working all the time on the Manor. Every now and then, they would hire some temporary help, but mostly it was just the two of 'em. After a few years, he invited an old widow to move into the Manor. Walter always felt it was his fault. The post office thing. Then he invited another and another.

From time to time a single old woman or old widower would move in. Walter and Learchman continued to add on to the place so we'd all have a place to live when we got old. I'm not sure if it was planned that way, but that's how it all worked out. You see, we thought we were doomed by looking into that mirror that day in the post office. Just the opposite happened. We vowed to never look into another mirror for the rest of our lives. Consequently we don't share any of our hours and our reflections never use our time."

Johnson continued, "Walter told us all about the mirror people. He said he talked to them. When he first told us of his exploits, we thought the old man has lost *his* marbles. Then he began to ask some of the older folks to move into the Manor. There was a hitch, of course. No mirrors.

We were told where we could go within the Manor, and some of the rules. Things like we had to keep ourselves healthy, and we had to be able to get along with the other residents. We couldn't bother Miss Emily, and we were never to talk of the mirrors again as long as he was alive. None of us thought his demands were very tough, and it *was* such a nice place. Everyone who was asked, moved into the Manor, and most have lived here ever since. Over the years, many of the residents have passed away. But you had to have an invitation to get in. We could never tell anyone on the outside what went on here. That was no big deal, mostly because we didn't know what went on here. I think Mr. Learchman was the construction foreman. He's been here longer than any resident. You already know some of us have been here for a very long time.

When Walter was alive, he was the one who invited the old townsfolk to join the Manor residents. Things changed after he died. This was just like any other old folks home, with the exception of no mirrors and, of course, Mr. Learchman. Once Walter died, Learchman controlled who lived here and who didn't. When someone died, Mr. Learchman took care of all of the arrangements. You see, we all started outliving our kids. So by the time we kick off, there will be no family here to take care of the arrangements. Consequently, Mr. Learchman takes care of all of those kinds of things."

I asked, "How did Walter die?"

Mr. Johnson looked surprised, "Well, he, ran out of hours."

Chapter Fifteen

Emma was *so* very punctual. I saw her walking up the street at about 7:50. I was sitting on the front porch of the Manor. It was already dark, and some of the residents had already gone to bed. Clara and Mr. Learchman were sitting on the porch with me when Emma arrived. The bite of winter was in the air, but it felt good to sit outside without all of the bugs of summer flying around. Clara was bundled up tightly with a jacket and a blanket. Once Emma climbed the steps, Mr. Learchman excused himself and went into the Manor and back to the front desk to maintain his vigil there.

"Emma." I asked, "So how was your day?"

"Fine." She said, She turned her attention to her Grandmother. "How are you, Grandma?"

Clara looked up from her lap and said. "Mr. Benson has kept us pretty entertained this evening. I am good sweetheart, and you, you are good?"

Emma glanced my way. "So Mr. Benson has been here a while?" I didn't know if she was asking me or Clara.

I said. "Yes, I have been here for a while. I had quite a talk with Mr. Johnson today, and Clara baked us some cookies. Isn't that right, Clara?"

She laughed with delight. "Do you know how long it has been since I baked cookies?" She thought for a moment and said. "Well it's been a long time, I'll tell ya." Emma looked my way and smiled.

We all went into the Manor, Clara felt proud and wanted Emma to have a cookie. You could see the love and admiration in Emma's eyes for her grandmother. We all went up the elevator and into Clara's apartment. She proceeded to the kitchen area of her place and took a plate down from the cupboard and added some cookies to it. She brought the plate to the living room and placed it on the coffee table.

"Would you like some tea or coffee?" she asked.

Emma said, "Let me help you. Tom, what would you like?"

I said, "Coffee, please."

Emma and Clara headed for the kitchen. The sun had set and lights from the city below were shining into the autumn night. I picked up a cookie and a magazine from the coffee table and glanced up to see if the women were looking. They were both scurrying around in the kitchen and talking as if they were alone. I noticed a film or cover on the windows. I hadn't noticed it earlier when it was full daylight, but now with the lights on in Clara's apartment, I could see it. I stood and began to walk toward the window.

Emma glanced my way and said, "Hey Tom, you still want your coffee black?"

I redirected to the kitchen and replied. "Black is fine for me." I noticed that I didn't see my reflection in the window. I must have been staring at the window when Clara said.

"Muslin."

I looked over and said, "I beg your pardon?"

Clara walked toward the window,   "Muslin is on the inside of the window. It helps keep the heat out in the summer and keeps the heat in during the winter." Clara watched me looking at the windows and the muslin covers.

She looked over to Emma and said. "Yes, Mr. Benson learned all kinds of things today. Isn't that right Mr. Benson?"

I looked back from the window and smiled.

"He knows about the shifters," she said softly to Emma.

Emma smiled to Clara. "He just thinks he knows about the shifters." Emma said it loud enough for me to overhear her comment to Clara.

Clara said. "You know, I haven't thought about them for years now. Well when you never use them, you don't think about 'em. After a while they just become an old thought. Sort of like air, you know it's there, you just don't notice."

Emma looked over to me. "Mr. Johnson told you all about the mirror people?" Her tone was more of a statement than a question. I knew I had to reply and didn't want to make a big deal about it.

I said, "Oh, we talked about a lot of things. Mr. Johnson has a lot of strange ideas." I didn't want to get Mr. Johnson in any trouble because of the things he revealed to me, or at least the ideas he planted.

"I guess you heard his version of the mirror people." Emma started as she returned to the living room. "To these people, it's like the urban legend of age. Some believe it so strong that they haven't seen a mirror for years."

I asked. "How 'bout you Emma, do you believe it? Believe that if you never look into another mirror, you will live forever?"

Emma was still smiling. "Is that what he told you? He said he thought he would never die?" She glanced back over to Clara and she just waved her hand as if to say, "I've already heard all of this, so you're on your own."

Emma went on, "Well you're smart enough to know that was wrong, right? You know everyone dies,

110

eventually. Mr. Johnson may have had some of his facts mixed up with some of his hopes. You know no one will live forever, I know you're that smart. Right."

"I never said I believed it all." I said. "I just wondered what you believed."

She said defensively. "Well I believe Beddington is a very nice place to be and I hope to be right here someday. Here in Beddington."

I smiled and nodded.

Emma paused and softened just a bit. "I've heard Mr. Johnson's story before, and quite frankly, I'd like to believe it. You know, sometimes when I look into a mirror, I can't believe the person looking back at me is me. That's happened to you, right, Tom?"

I began to answer but she cut me off and went on,

"Like the other night we went out and I drank a little." She quickly glanced over to Clara to see if she was paying attention to her conversation with me. She was.

Emma went on, "The next morning I woke up early, because I had to work the morning shift, and when I looked into the mirror, I could have sworn it was not my reflection staring back at me."

I took notice that Emma said the word reflection, just like Mr. Johnson pointed out a number of times. He said that the people who knew stopped thinking of themselves being in the mirror. They knew it was only a reflection and referred to the reflection as that.

"So having known all about this urban legend," Emma continued, "I just blow it off, take my shower and take another look after I dry off. I double check and yep it's me, most of the time.

Have you ever looked into the mirror, Tom, and said to yourself, I've got to get into shape?"

I sucked in my gut almost out of a reflex.

Emma noticed and said, "I don't mean you're not in shape, but have you ever looked into the mirror and said that to yourself, or I need to color my hair or maybe just had the thought, well, anything negative about the way you look?"

I continued the pressure for her to commit. "So you do believe it all, then? The things Mr. Johnson said?"

Emma shifted in her chair, "You know there's no proof? This is all just a theory, a legend. Something to keep all the townsfolk talking. It's all part of the mystery of Beddington." I thought she was going to confirm Mr. Johnson's story.

She turned, looked at Clara and then back again to me. "And how could you prove it, prove something like the mirrors having

any consequence on a person's age?" I was becoming more and more interested. I wanted to look into a mirror. Emma stood up and moved to the kitchen to retrieve another cup of coffee.

"You see Tom," She continued, "according to legend, the reflection in the mirror, is not simply a reflection, it's another world. A world where the people or reflections or things or whatever you want to call them, live in the mirrors. Once we die, you will never see that reflection again, which makes perfect sense. Anyway they call them shiftees or shifters mainly because they can shift their appearance."

I replied. "That's sort of what Mr. Johnson told me."

This began the flood of information, it was like Emma wanted me to know. Even Clara had a different look on her face.

Emma went on, "You see, each window is different, some mirrors have a few shiftees and some have a lot. You generally don't have your own shiftee that follows you around from mirror to mirror. They call them windows, we call them mirrors. They do exactly what we do when we are in front of the mirror about 99.99% of the time. It's that other .01% that Mr. Beddington detected."

Clara sat and examined each of Emma's words to make sure the story was correct. She piped in. "And not to mention the post office fiasco."

Emma added. "Yes, the day time caught up with everyone. No one noticed that no one had aged, I mean, the people simply didn't notice. There was nothing to remind them they were getting older. No morning routine that they had to go through. No looking in the mirror to see if they looked good enough to go slop the hogs or milk the cows. The people just went and did their work. And in all reality, you really don't notice how or if you change each and every day you look into a mirror. About 99% of the way we feel is pretty much determined by the way we look, or at least the way we think we look. After a while, no one even missed the mirrors. As time went on and some of the people moved to other parts of the country, we lost contact with most of 'em, but some of the ones who were still here, I mean in Twodot, moved right into the Manor. Mr. Beddington felt horrible to have his friends and relatives age like they did, simply by looking into a mirror. Mr. Beddington moved what mirrors that were left into his basement."

I interrupted her, asking, "I thought Mrs. Beddington destroyed all of the mirrors in the post office?"

"Not all," she went on, "She broke one and then she just cried and cried. Mr. Beddington was down there for years studying the mirrors. According to some of the people who were supposed to know, Walter Beddington continued to order mirror after mirror from back east, always thinking that he may have just received bad mirror after another, and of course, Emily had smashed only one of them in the post office.

"When Walter and Emily went into seclusion for a few years, it seemed like Walter became obsessed with the mirrors. That's when he ordered all of the others. He ordered mirrors from all of the world. One by one they came in on the train. Mr. Learchman was in town constantly to pick them up. He never said much, and no one ever talked to him. Well, of course, everyone in town thought Walter and Emily went nuts.

After they came out of seclusion, they started to invite some of their friends to move into the Manor to live with them. When their families came to visit, Walter and Learchman told the little kids they could play in the basement. Anyway, I guess he ran test after test, mostly on the kids, nothing bizarre. He just let the kids look into the mirror for hours at a time. Nothing really became of his tests. As far as we know, those kids went on to lead normal lives. However, all of the kids we do know of haven't lived past sixty or seventy years old. I guess some of them are still alive, but like I said, we've lost contact with most of 'em.

Walter, obsessed with longevity, began to do the math, and discovered the formula for long life. That equation didn't include mirrors. He always felt the mirrors had a large part to do with our longevity especially when he discovered that we all share our hours with the shifters. He decided that people could live without mirrors and, once he shared that information with some of his friends, and they spread the word. Well, we knew we didn't want to have or be around a mirror or any other reflective device."

Clara added, "Muslin," and pointed to the windows. Clara continued, "We still go outside and we still even go into town once in a while. We're not afraid. We've just done without mirrors for so long, and we're doing so well, we figured, what the heck, don't knock a good thing."

I had to ask, "How exactly did Walter figure out that we share our life with the shifters?"

"Well." Clara began. "Walter said he talked to the shifters. He said he crossed into their world and they told him all about how we get just so many hours and that we need to share with them, so they can live as well."

I glanced over to Emma, wanting some kind of confirmation. She met my look with rolled eyes.

Clara went on, "Walter said that every time we stand in front of the mirror, we give our energy to the shifters. That's why we lose some of our hours and they gain energy and are always there when we walk into any room with a mirror."

The story Emma and Clara were spinning was almost too good to be a fake. This was pretty much what Mr. Johnson had said as well. They had too many details. And quite frankly, it all sounded feasible. Well, at least it sounded like they believed it.

I had to ask. "Emma, how did you learn about all of this? You know, I have been around for quite some time and I have never heard this urban legend. Do you think this is just a local thing? Maybe a myth?

Emma replied, "These people live it every day. I haven't even started with the details Tom. You see, we don't talk about it. No one really wants to believe it, but most of them feel they are the living proof. Proof that you can live without mirrors and will live longer that way."

The tension was heavy in the room. We could all feel it and I wanted to lighten things up a little so I recounted my story of the bathroom on the first floor, Clara and Emma both laughed a little.

"The shiftees were just having some fun with you." Clara said. "They probably didn't mean to scare you. We all seem to be afraid of things we don't understand."

I continued. "So you mean each time I look into a mirror, I'm losing years from my life?" I continued. "And every time I look into a mirror, it's really not my reflection, it is an alien from another world? Is that right?"

Emma started. "Well sort of, but on the positive side, you don't count your sleep time, or at least that is how the legend goes."

Clara added. "Unless you have a mirror in your bedroom." Emma laughed. "You can live without the mirror, and really, even though we believe it's another world, we really don't believe they're aliens. I mean, get real, aliens?"

It was getting late and Clara was beginning to doze off every now and again. Emma noticed and said,

"Grandma, we are going to have to be leaving, is there anything we can do for you before we take off?"

Clara smiled and waved us toward the door. We all stood up and moved toward the front door. I thanked Clara. "You have been such a big help."

She looked up and said. "You'll get it, son." I nodded and she smiled as she herded Emma and me out the door.

As we were standing in the hallway, I reached over and gave Emma a little kiss on the cheek.

"Thank you Emma, you're quite a woman." I said.

She smiled and said. "Thanks yourself, I think you're quite a guy. Do you want your mirror education now?"

"Oh, I thought I just got it." I said surprised. "Is there more?"

"Have you been wondering what happened to all of those mirrors? She asked. You know, when they outlawed mirrors in the town? Or how Walter did all of his testing or where he did all of his testing? You already saw one of his mirrors."

I immediately thought of the men's room on the first floor. "Yeah…" is all I could say to that. "So what are you trying to say? You know where all of

Walter's mirrors are? I just assumed he would have destroyed them all."

Emma had the cutest smile, "Nope, he didn't destroy any of them. They're all still here. They're in the basement. No one lives down there. Remember, women on the 2nd floor and men on the 1st. No one is on the basement level. That was always off limits. That is where Walter kept all of his mirrors."

I said, "I can't believe they are still down there. Do the townspeople know?"

Emma looked back at me. "Remember Tom, it's been a long time since that post office day. Most of those people are either living right here, dead, or gone. It's like an amusement park down there. C'mon, we'll take the back stairs."

I followed Emma like a little puppy dog. I never hesitated to be able to see the things that the residents of this house were afraid of. I thought Emma was great. We walked down the back stairs and took the second flight down to the basement. The main entrance was locked. Emma, somehow, had a key to the main door. When I looked over her shoulder, she glanced back and said. "Don't ask." I didn't.

Chapter Sixteen

The door opened upon a dark but impressive grand ballroom. The hall lights gave an eerie feel to the room. It looked like a ghost convention. White sheets and dust covers were thrown over hundreds of mirrors. We wandered through the room for a minute or two just to absorb the grandness of it all. Emma located a light switch and flipped it.

The room came alive as the light flooded the ghost- filled ballroom. We both stopped. What seemed to be the amusement park had suddenly turned hard and cold. We were both snapped back into the reality of the unknown. The mysterious ghost shapes had changed into the dusty-grey sheets over the mirrors.

I asked Emma. "Have you ever been down here before?"

She looked back to me. "I was one of them." She paused, turned away from me and walked further into the room. I followed her and touched her arm.

"What?" I said.

"I was one of those kids Walter experimented with. I loved this room." She began to dance around the room. "We never thought it was an experiment, we thought it was just a place to play while our parents visited our relatives. We never even noticed that Walter was always here."

"So you knew Walter?" I asked.

"Sure, he was just a worker here, he was like Learchman. He directed the construction of the building, he helped all of the grandparents. And he played with all of us. The kids didn't really know he was Mr. Beddington at the time, we just called him Walter.

"Each week he had the mirrors lined up a different way. It was always fun to find a new mirror arrangement. One time he would have the mirrors across from each other and the other times he would have them lined up, one after the other. He had them in a big circle one time, so that when you stood in the middle, you see yourself from every angle. You could dance or pretend to play cowboys and Indians or you could do anything you wanted while you were here in the mirrors.

"One day he had all of the mirrors lined up against the far walls. We all had to stand back as far as we could and then walk toward them. Then we went back to the wall and ran to the mirrors, each time we had to touch the mirrors when we got real close to them. After we played in the mirrors for a while, he would always have milk and cookies for us. We had little rugs we laid out on the floor. Sometimes we all took a nap, right here on the floor.

"I didn't figure it out until years later that he was trying to figure out a way to get into the mirrors. He was using us to find the way in." She stopped and turned back to me. "He must have found a way in. He always had this one mirror that he would never let any of the kids play with. It was always really big and was turned to the wall."

She was looking around the room, and began to head for one of the covered mirrors across the room.

"This is the one," she said, indicating the largest mirror in the room. "He never let us touch this one or play with it or even look into it. She pulled the cover off. The mirror was at least eight foot tall and five feet wide. It was framed in the most beautiful wooden carving I had ever seen. Every figure was like a mirrored image to itself. There were people face to face and back to back. There were children head to head and toe to toe. It was an awesome carving.

I said to Emma, "This should be in a museum." I joined her in front of the mirror. The glass looked old and worn. I put my hand up to the mirror and it sank in. I pulled it back, amazed and looked at my hand and then at Emma. She smiled from ear to ear and did the same. Sunk her arm into the mirror up to her elbow. She pulled it out and started laughing.

"Tom, Tom, Tom" she said almost screaming. "Do you know what we've got?" She was very excited, jumping around, and I had to admit I didn't know exactly what we had.

She said, "We have the window to another world." I put my hand back up to the mirror, and stood on the side so I could see both front and back. I inserted my hand into the mirror and checked out the back and to my amazement, the back was solid and flat. I pulled my hand out again and backed up a little, looked over to Emma and the smile was stuck on her face.

Emma, watching me, said. "I'm going in."

I cranked my head towards her and said. "Are you kidding? You don't know what will happen when you get in there. You don't know if you can…" I paused, "come back."

She pushed up her sleeves and looked directly into the mirror. "Coming?" As she turned her head to me, she already had her hands up to the front of the mirror.

She had not heard a thing I said. "Emma, Emma…" I turned to see her eye to eye. "I have to" she said. We both looked back into the mirror.

I glanced at her in the mirror, "Yep, let's go."

Chapter Seventeen

Emma stepped into the mirror like she had done it a hundred times. I was a little less confident of our new endeavor. As Emma went through, I could still see her on the other side of the mirror. She turned back for a second and looked over her shoulder straight at me. Her mouth formed the words, "Come on Tom," but the mirror seemed to swallow the sound. She motioned for me to follow and then simply disappeared. I stopped and just stared into the mirror.

Had I been imagining this whole endeavor? Was this just a mirror?

Emma re-appeared in the mirror and startled me. This was not my imagination. She again motioned for me to follow. Reluctantly I took the plunge. Once inside the mirror, I again saw Emma just standing there, waiting for me. As we moved into the mirror, we stepped into a long dark hallway. It was a world of, what now appeared to be blackened hallways lined with windows. We turned back to the mirror we had just entered and I saw the room we had just been in. There was Learchman, heading straight toward the mirror. We both stopped to watch. Learchman gazed at what now appeared to be a window and smiled to himself. I thought he was smiling at us. I waved, but he didn't acknowledge me. I glanced over to Emma, she didn't wave. She was just watching *me*. Learchman picked up the white dust cover from the floor and placed it over the mirror Emma and I had just walked through, until all I saw was the white sheet. After a minute or two, the window went black.

He must have turned out the lights to the room. I wondered why Learchman hadn't acknowledged us in the mirror.

Unfazed, Emma turned away from the entrance, taking a step.

"Do you think he saw us?" I asked.

She took my hand. "Maybe, but it doesn't really matter. Does it?"

Once on the other side the mirror, I could see long hallways leading away from us both left and right. This side was darker than the other. There were figures moving all over the place. Each figure looked the same. All were faceless and appeared to be wearing a silver skin-tight outfit. They only resembled a person in height and stature. Some were standing directly in front and some were standing to the side of each window. Many were moving from one window to the next.

It seemed like we were invisible for not a single one of these people stopped to ask us a thing. They were not aggressive, however, they moved as if they had a purpose.

As we moved about this surreal world of seemingly endless hallways and rooms, everything was very quiet. No normal noise. You know, like the kind of noise people make as they go about their daily living. Even our own footsteps made no noise. It was like the walls absorbed the sound. The only visible light was that, that filtered in from the windows. The smell was old, like stagnant air. Little, if any circulation.

There were windows everywhere, and I guessed every window was a mirror on the other side.

All sizes and shapes. Some of the windows were high and some appeared to be at floor level. I could see each window, but when I went close to look out of them, I sort of passed through a clear membrane. I could look out the window to see a room and if I turned around I could see the same room reflected behind me but without me in it. It was sort of two-dimensional, and once back through the membrane, I assumed the people on the other side of the mirror could no longer see me. If that was the case, I now understood why Learchman didn't see us. We were past the membrane. Wow, this was great. I could see people through each window, and because I didn't pass through the membrane, they couldn't see me. This must have been what Mr. Johnson was talking about when he said 'If they did everything we din then we wouldn't want to go the their side.'

We tried to talk to some of the figures, but they all acted as if they were far too busy to talk to us. I had no idea what these beings were. Emma called them the shiftees. When I got the attention of one of them, they went into the routine of doing the same things I did. They mouthed the same words I said, however they made no noise, they only moved their lips as if they were talking. It was like they couldn't understand that we were on their side of the window. They weren't alone. I couldn't understand how we could be on this side either.

Still holding Emma's hand, she said, "Remember what John said? It's not you, it's just your reflection. I looked from the figure in front of me over to Emma. "This isn't my reflection." I said.

Emma's eyes moved back to the figure. She pointed at the figure with her chin. When I looked forward again, I was face to face with my reflection. The figure in front of me had changed from the silver being, to an identical copy of me. By reflex, I took a step back. Then I raised my hand as if I was standing in front of a mirror. I reached forward to touch the duplicate of myself. His hand met mine. We both smiled. At least I smiled and he followed. I pulled my hand back as if I had touched something hot.

I took Emma's hand, moved to the side of the figure in front of me and continued down the hall. The figure I left behind, still mimicking me, changed from my likeness back to the silver form we stopped just a minute ago. He turned and moved in the opposite direction.

As we passed more of the windows, I could see the silver figures moving past the membrane, taking the form of the person on the other side. Once the person moved out of mirror range, the silver clad figures moved behind the membrane. They just stood there and kept looking out the window, and they shifted back into the silver image again. The larger the window, the more shifters there were, always alert.

As we moved through the eerie silence I could see an endless array of windows and even more shifters always on standby, always ready. Shifters were continually moving in and out of the membrane to mimic the people on the other side. I could see the people on the other side of the window, each one a stranger to me. "Do you know who that is?" I asked Emma. She shook her head. I asked the next time we saw someone. Again she shook her head. At the next window, I just pointed, she said, "No." Some of the people were brushing their teeth, some were taking a shower and some were just staring into the mirror. I am sure they all thought they were just looking at themselves or at least their reflections. The people on the outside, looking into their mirrors had no idea that this world existed. They thought they were alone in their bathrooms or bedrooms, or at least they never thought anyone could see them from the other side of their own private mirror. We glanced at each window as we passed. As I passed one window, a woman was looking into the side of the mirror. She turned her head as we walked by, like she was watching us. It occurred to me as we passed that window, the woman looked familiar. It wasn't until some time later it registered, Kate Slybeck. I stopped and ran back to that window. The room was empty.

Emma inquired, I just said I thought I saw someone I knew.

It appeared that the figures that were posted at their windows never left that station. Others moved from window to window, some just passing by and others stopped at each window to look. If the figures that were posted at that window were already engaged the moving figures stayed at that window until the others were back. If there was no activity, they move on to the next window.

I remembered that Clara had said that Walter Beddington talked to 'them'. She had to have meant the people in the mirrors. She told me that Walter had crossed over and talked to them. They told Walter about how the shifters subtracted years, or at least hours from your life. The shifters that were standing in front of each window on standby were not talking and the others that moved from window to window were also silent. So I knew there still had to be someone or something we hadn't seen yet. The shifters never took their face away from the window and some of the faceless figures that noticed us, continued on their assigned pattern of duties.

As we continued, we ran into more crowded hallways, some of the figures had faces now. We hadn't seen these figures with faces earlier, so it was a little bit of a shock. I thought this may be the next generation of shiftees or some other order. Whatever they were, they had human faces and silver bodies. Once they arrived at the window, the shifter that was mimicking the human slipped back into the membrane and the shifter with a face took over the duty of following the human in the mirror.

Have you ever looked into a mirror and said to yourself, wow, this a bad mirror? You look into the mirror and the reflection is different than what you thought it should be. That always happens when you don't like the reflection. I discovered that sometimes you don't get your assigned shifter. Sometimes you get a generic shifter or just a regular shifter. You just think it's a bad mirror. That's just what they want you to think.

As the hallways came together, it opened up to a giant Hub with hundreds of hallways leading to who knew where. It appeared to be like the Denver International Airport on the day before Christmas. Figures going every which way, some with faces, some without.

Emma took my hand. "Could we get lost?" Her concern surprised me since she had been so eager to embark on our journey.

Though I assured her, "Don't worry, I know the way back." I thought to myself that we should have left a bread crumb trail. We walked around the central area and could see concourse after concourse of silver figures moving and changing locations. Entering membranes and stepping back and moving on to a new location and waiting on this side of the next membrane. All moved in silence. It was like the window was a sound barrier. The noise from the outside world didn't get into this one either. The shifters nor the roamers talked or made any noise as they moved about.

In the middle of the hub, where all of the hallways came together, there appeared to be a very large column. We walked up to it, full of apprehension. Upon closer inspection, I saw the large column had doors. I had been so enthralled by my new surroundings that I hadn't noticed that there were no doors anywhere along the hallways. I could not see the ceiling, either. Everything was very dark except for the light that entered the windows.

The column in the center of the core shot up so high that it eventually faded to black. We didn't know if these doors lead into something or maybe it was the way out, but we did know we had to find out.

Trepidation overwhelmed us as we tried each door. There were no apparent locks or handles. This column was built in the shape of a very large octagon with multiple doors on each wall. We pushed on each door, to no avail. There was no give to any of the doors. We started knocking and hammering on each one. Finally one opened.

I was looking at myself face to face. My other self said, "Hello, Mr. Benson, Miss Sorensen, would you like to come in?"

I am sure I had a shocked look on my face as I said. "Who are you, and why do you look like me?" This was the first voice we heard. This figure was not like the figures in the halls. This was more than just my reflection. Up until now, the figures we had seen made no noise. No conversation. The figure behind the door didn't mimic me. My mirror image said nothing at first. We entered the room, and I could hardly take my eyes off the other me. He was completely three dimensional just like me. I pulled my eyes away and took a quick look around. This room was like the opposite of the dark hallways. The room was lit up like daylight. There were thousands of these beings in the multi-tiered room, levels as high as you could see, filled with these beings, all monitoring some type of computer system, the likes I had never seen. They all had multiple screen and they moved the screens around simply by waving their hands. They typed some kind of commands without a keyboard. It looked like they were typing or making gestures in the air. The screens in front of them moved constantly.

This room was similar to Beddington Manor, in that it appeared to be much larger on the inside than on the outside. As I looked at all of these foreign beings, each one of them had my face and were wearing my clothes. Emma caught my eye and she tried to cover her nervousness with a half smile to me.

My other self said, "We are what you understand,"

"Well I certainly *do not* understand this," I said.

With a wave of his hand all of the me's changed to look like Emma.

I smiled and Emma grabbed my hand and squeezed. "Don't let me go." The smile left her face. The other me waved his hand again and all of the figures changed to the faceless people of the hallway.

He smiled and began to explain. "We are the changers. You have been given a unique opportunity to meet us. We do not allow too many people from your side to ours. As you can see, there are many of us. Our existence is based on your world. There is one of us for every one of you."

As we talked to the now, silver changer we began to walk the parameter of the room. The spiral path rose and circled all of the workers who were sending and receiving messages over what appeared to some kind of wireless computers. I thought back to the computer in the interview room at the Manor. The first interview with Clara. The computer screen was filled with her side of our conversation. I thought, at the time, it was the things she said, now I wondered if it was the things she read.

Chapter Eighteen

"Who were the people in the hall?" I asked. "What is a changer?"

The changer began, "The forms in front of the transports are shifters. They have the ability to shift into any shape. The others are roamers. They assist the shifters. If there is a need. The faced forms are special roamers."

He didn't explain their specialty.

He continued, "When someone is born on your side of the world, someone is born here also."

A million thoughts were flooding my mind, and I asked, "Why us?" He seemed to know that I wanted to know why they were sharing this with us.

He didn't hesitate. "You found the way in. There are many ways to get here, and even more ways to get back, you found your way here. Some people get in to our side and yet never find their way here, you did." He smiled and waited for a response.

"And so because we found our way in, you're going to share the world secrets with us?" I smiled back.

Calmly he replied, "Not really, just some of the things that might make your life better. I can tell you how it all works."

"How what works?" I asked.

"Your life," he said and glanced back at the screens behind him, hit a few air keys and turned back to us again.

Emma was squeezing my hand, standing a little behind me.

Then looking at our guide she asked. "What about me? Can you tell me how my life works, too?"

The changer looked over to Emma. "They all work pretty much the same." He reacted to our surprised look with one of his own surprised mirrored faces. "Sometimes I am surprised about how much you humans don't know. You are the blessed species and you don't even know it. You are the only species that get a million hours. You did know that, right?

Emma looked over to me, nodded and raised her eyebrows as if I was to confirm his assumption.

The changer continued as we walked on. "From the day you're born until the day you die, you can use one million hours. Actually you're allowed a million, and only your waking hours count."

I had already done the math on this after my conversation with Mr. Johnson. "That's about 170 years." I said.

"Very good, Mr. Benson. Actually it is 171 years, two months, twenty days and four hours, your time."

I looked over to Emma, raised my eyebrows, looking for acknowledgement. She smiled and re-fixed her eyes on our silver guide.

"Most humans are not so lucky to live that long, and there are many variables. You lose hours when you are self-destructive."

He stopped and turned back to us and said, "Most of you are so destructive. Of course some

people sleep more than others. Some have more bad
habits that others."

"Are those the only variables?" I asked.

"Transactions." He said, "some of you have so
many transactions".

"Transactions?" I inquired.

"Yes, each time you look into a mirror, we call
that a transaction." He went on, "For each hour of
time you look at yourself in a mirror, you give up one
of your hours, and for each hour of transaction we
observe, that would be you in front of any mirror at
any time, we receive the bonus time."

I asked. "And that 'bonus time' what is that,
what do you get from that?" Without hesitation, he
said. "It allows us time...time in your world." He
paused, observed the confusion on our faces and went
on.

"You see, when you look into a mirror, your
reflection tells you who you are. It tells you if you are
big or small, young or old, fat or skinny. Well, you get
the picture. We are the ones that tell you not only *who*
you are but *how* you are as well. When you look into a
mirror, you use us to judge yourself." He continued,
"Our world is binding, not like yours. We have very
little geography to cross.

"We have limits here. The mirror you look
into at home may be right next to the mirror you look
into on the 8th floor restroom next to your office, Mr.
Benson. At the very least, our windows are right next
to each other. Little geography to cross."

I protested. "No geography? There are people,
well shifters and roamers moving all over the place
out there." He changed back to my reflection instantly

and had the look of excitement on his face, or on my face, or what looked like my face. I calmed.

He continued, "We are bound by the walls and windows you see here. Shifters and roamers never leave this place. The shifters are assigned to one mirror, their job is to shift into any image that comes to that mirror. The roamers move from one location to another per our commands. You see, we monitor your every move. From here we can tell what location you are at and where your assigned roamer needs to be. We know which mirrors you go to regularly and we always have either your assigned roamer, a regular roamer, or a shifter there. Anyway, back to your question. What do we do in your world?

Have you ever had a friend say he saw you at this place or that place, and you knew you weren't there? You say 'It wasn't me, must have been someone else.' Your friend scratches his head and says 'It sure looked like you.' Well that was one of us!

"When one of your friends say 'Hey I met your twin last week.

You say 'Wrong-o big boy, I don't have a twin'. That was one of us also.

"You blow it off to either bad eyesight, or you think your friend may have had too much to drink. To be in your world is exhilarating. It feels like total freedom for us. You are not bound by walls and windows. You can go outside, you can choose to not look into a window or a mirror. You can eat.

That is what the bonus time is used for. To be in your world. Even though it is only for a little while, it is very sought after. Only a few are selected to have that honor.

This could also explain why some mornings you still feel so tired. You see, it takes a lot of energy to be in your world. Also, we can only be in your world while you are sleeping. If you saw yourself . . . well, it wouldn't be good." His body transformed back to silver.

I asked. "Is that what you're here for, to invade our world?"

Our guide just smiled. "No, Mr. Benson, our purpose is to learn about you and make you feel better about yourself. Our excursions into your world are like ... like your vacations."

I said, "Let me get this clear, your job is to make me feel better about myself? What difference does it make to you and your world how I feel about myself?"

"We are the same, you and me. Actually you and your assigned roamer are the same. You are connected.

"Connected? How?" I said puzzled.

Right then all of the doors to the internal column opened and a roamer entered each door. We had been strolling along the path around the room and were already twenty or thirty feet above the floor and doors we had entered. I looked down and to my amazement all of the roamers looked exactly like me. As I was looking, they all began to fade back to chrome. All but one, who continued to look like me. It had to be my assigned roamer. He just waved to me. I waved back uncertainly and turned back to the controller.

"It is just our purpose, it is the plan, you're never alone. We've been doing this since time began, it is how things are done." He concluded.

"What happens now?" I asked. He was looking at me as his face went from the chrome metal I had almost become used to seeing now back to my reflection. "This isn't the first time you've been here and it won't be the last Tom Benson. For now, you go back." He said. The controller simply lifted his hand before I could respond and the next thing I knew I was staring at myself in the bathroom mirror of my hotel room.

Chapter Nineteen

I looked at my watch on the vanity. It was 3 a.m. and I was still in my wrinkled clothes from the day before. Feeling a little groggy, I took a sip of water and wandered to the bed, took off my shirt and got in. I laid there for just a minute before springing back to an upright position and leaping from the bed. I quickly looked at the bed to see if I had been in the bed all night or just got in. I ran to the bathroom and looked into the mirror I had just been staring into. I raised my hand, fully expecting to sink back into the glass. My hand stopped at the front of the mirror. I moved my hand around all over the mirror looking for the soft spot. It was not there. I was back into my own world. I sneered at my reflection and returned to my room. My first tendency was to call Emma. I ran to the phone, picked it up and began to dial. I stopped before I had finished. What if Emma wasn't there or what if she hadn't even been with me at all? What if I hadn't really been there? What if the whole thing was just a dream? I turned around to look at the bed again. I was sure it had been slept in, for how long I couldn't tell, but it looked like I had been running a marathon in my sleep. And yet I knew I had been somewhere else tonight.

I began to pace the floor. I had to get this down on paper or maybe into the computer so I didn't forget it. So I *wouldn't* forget it. I sat down at the desk, turned the laptop on and began to type. I typed the rest of the night, or should I say the rest of the morning. I put it down just as I remembered it. The giant mirror doorway. The hallways and windows. The people in the hallways, the membrane, looking through the windows. The controllers, changing from the silver form to look like me and then like Emma and back to silver. The million hours. All of the shifters, and the roamers and the changers and the...

When I woke up, I was still sitting in front of the laptop. The computer was still on and I already forgotten why I was here instead of the bed. I stood up and stretched and hit the return key on the laptop. I began to read the fifteen pages that I had typed just hours ago. It all came back to me. I looked at the clock and it was already 8 a.m. I remembered most of the items on the pages, but wasn't sure now if it was all a dream or if it was real. I needed to talk to Emma. I held off the temptation to call until I had my shower. As I was drying off, I returned to the computer and hooked up the printer, and printed off a copy of the file. I called Emma at nine sharp. Fearing all of this could have been in my head or maybe just a dream, and convincing myself I was not crazy, I didn't blast away into Emma's peaceful morning. I instead only asked how she was doing and if she was all right.

She said she was still very tired. "Had a rough night, tossed and turned all night. Not too restful when you do that, ya know? And I had the strangest dream again. I have had such strange dreams ever since I met you, Tom. What have you done to me?"

I said, "Nothing bad, I hope. Emma, can you come over? We need to talk."

She said, "Tom, I just woke up. Can we make it in an hour?"

I said, "This is important, I'll come to you."

She hesitated a little, but said,

"Okay, now?"

"Right now." I said.

We hung up the phone and I was on my way, the paper file in my hand. I arrived at Emma's just fifteen minutes later. She had just crawled out of the shower and answered the door in her robe with a towel in hand and drying her hair. She was doing that hair flip thing.

Anyway, I said "You know that dream you had last night? Do you remember it?" I sat her down at her kitchen table and handed her the file I was carrying.

Emma read through page after page of the recorded events from the previous night. She looked up several times and cupped her hand over her mouth. While she was reading, I refilled our coffee cups.

She looked up after a couple of pages and said, "This is my dream." I didn't have time to respond before she was right back into it.

She completed the last page and lifted her face to mine.

I asked, "Did you know about this? Did you know this could happen? Have you ever done that before?"

She said, "The last thing I remember was saying good-night to Clara and taking you to the basement at Beddington. The next thing was waking up to your phone call."

"I thought this was a dream Tom." She said as she waved the pages of last nights account at me. "Is it possible we both had the same dream? And yes, I've had similar dreams, but it was a long time ago."

I asked, "Do you remember playing in the mirror room with Walter Beddington?"

"Of course, I remember playing around in the mirrors, but nothing ever happened. Nothing like last night. Nothing I can remember. And besides, what would be the point of sending kids into the mirror?" She said and her voice faded on the last word.

I sat down at the kitchen table across from her. "Wasn't there any talk about Walter? I mean it seems like he was sort of an odd duck. Going in to seclusion, building this mansion, bringing in Learchman.

Emma stared off into nothing for a minute. She took a sip of her coffee and began. "There were stories that Walter made numerous trips into the mirror. Clara would tell me things she heard like the changers shared more with him than just information. She said that taught him things. Walter learned the secret of building in the 4th dimension from the mirror people according to her. I always listened but dismissed it as just another Clara story. Have you noticed the size of the Manor?

"You know, I made a note the first day I saw the manor. I thought it was bigger on the inside."

She said, "I think he provided the children to the changers. The kids would eventually wake up and think it was all just a dream."

"What adult would believe such a story?" Emma questioned.

I proposed the idea, "Maybe another trade off was now the old folks. I mean if they never looked into a mirror, while they may live longer, they had no need for shifters, roamers or changers. That meant more of them could cross over into our world. For vacation? And if they could copy us, we could never tell just by looking at them, right?"

Emma looked as if she was contemplating my question. I asked her, "Can you remember some of your old dreams? You know, like when you were a kid?" Emma was trying to recall some of the memories that were either lost or locked into her sub conscience. She was gazing into the distance.

She started, "I remember that playing in the mirror room we were never afraid. We laughed at the old people, because none of them had mirrors in their rooms. We thought they were scared of the mirrors. Walter was the only one that wasn't afraid. The first time he took us to the basement, he put his finger to is lips and said 'Shhh, don't tell them." He pointed up to the next floor. Then he opened the door to the mirror room.

"He took us on trips." The look on her face changed and she jerked her head toward me as she forced herself to realize. "*He* took us into the mirror! It seemed like it was just another day playing. I think we played with the shifters. I think sometimes the shifters or maybe the changers would come back and play outside with us. Hell, we were just kids, what'd we know? We grew up thinking this was normal. You know, kids thinking and talking about their imaginary friends. Your parents never believed anything you said, anyway. I think I must have had a real friend in the mirror. We all did, so all of us kids looked forward to going to the Manor. It meant we could play with our friends . . . always."

I asked her, "Well, if the changers came back here to play with you, how did they get back to the ... the other side?"

"Well, I guess because they were the reflection, when they looked into a mirror, they didn't get another reflection back. They could just enter any mirror, I guess. I never really thought about it much then. We would be outside playing and the next thing I'd knew, we'd be in my room and she was waving goodbye. She would be on the other side of the mirror and always wave back. She always had a tear in her eye when she had to leave." Emma was gazing again, like she was reliving each moment.

"And Learchman was there. Learchman was always there to help the kids. When I first met Learchman he didn't talk much."

Another revelation came to Emma.

"Oh my God, he's a changer, Tom!"

Chapter Twenty

As we sat there together, I think we both came to the realization that this was so much bigger than the age of some of the people at the Beddington Manor. We had come across a situation that we could neither explain nor prove. All we really had was our personal knowledge that there was something going on with the mirrors. We knew the truth, but had no way to prove any of it. We agreed also that we had to consider what we would accomplish if we could prove what we thought we knew. After all, these beings or images were not really out to hurt us or hurt anyone for that matter. They simply wanted to spend time outside the mirror. At least, that's what we were told.

Emma began to tell me about when she was a child. She said for as long as she could remember, Learchman was always around.

She said, "Thinking about it now, he really has never aged. I never thought about it much, but you know, when you see someone all the time, you sort of stop looking at them. I have never seen him outside the Manor. He was always there to help Walter Beddington, and when Walter passed on, it was Learchman who took care of Emily."

We decided we needed to get back into the mirror. There were many unanswered questions. Like who is Learchman? What is he doing here? Why do the mirror people want to come to our side and do the mirrors really make any difference in our ageing process? We wanted to wait until dark took over the Manor. I didn't want to be too conspicuous by trudging to the basement in the middle of the day. Emma pointed out, that none of the residents would want to follow us, because they knew what was down there.

That night we met at the Manor at 10 p.m. All of the lights from the residents' rooms were out. The soft lighting was on in the hallway. We decided to go to the rear of the building even though Learchman was not at the desk, because we thought it would be more discrete to use the back entrance. To our surprise, the door was secured for the night. We looked at each other and almost laughed.

We looked around for a window to climb into. And decided to check out the cellar door. To our relief, it was open and the stairs were lit. Once we returned to the lower level of the Manor, we went directly to the room of mirrors. We went to the

146

entrance mirror, pulled the sheet from it, and looked at each other.

She said, "Ready?"

I said, "Let's go."

Emma put her hand to the mirror and her hand stopped there. She glanced back to me with a surprised look on her face. She began to try again by putting both hands in front of the mirror. She smiled at me and started forward, only to be stopped again by the glass. I put my hand to the glass and it was as solid as it could be. The reflections followed our every move and we couldn't trip them up. They did their job per design. We both felt all over the mirror and there were no soft spots and we clearly would not enter through this mirror tonight.

I look to Emma and said, "Was this a dream?" She just continued to look into the mirror and just shook her head.

I could see movement from the corner of my eye I turned to see Learchman walking up behind us. I wasn't sure how to act. We were both facing Learchman with our backs to the mirror.

Learchman spoke first, "What are you doing here?" Learchman was always to the point.

I said, "We were just checking out some of these mirrors. How much do you know about all of these mirrors, Mr. Learchman?" He walked behind the mirror and picked up the white sheet and placed it back over the mirror.

"You are not supposed to be here." He pointed to the door and motioned for us both to leave.

Emma touched his arm and said, "William, do you remember the games we used to play down here years ago?" He softened instantly; a smile came to his face. She continued, "Do you remember Walter and all the fun things he showed us?" Learchman was nodding his head as he was listening to Emma. She walked around him, always touching him. "Do you remember us going into the mirror? William, do you?" His eyes followed her around.

"You were little then" he shined.

"Would you like to go into the mirror with us, William?"

His smile disappeared. "I never go into the mirror, I never go. I keep all mirrors covered now. I cannot go in the mirrors." Learchman became very agitated and moved toward me in an aggressive nature. I backed up immediately. Emma stopped him with another touch of her hand to his.

While their backs were turned to the mirror, I slid behind the mirror and again removed the cover. I slowly moved in front and gazed into the mirror.

Emma and William were talking when I blurted out, "Oh my God." They both turned around and I heard Emma gasp as she saw what I was looking at.

Through the mirror, I could see Emma and myself. I could not see Learchman, and Emma's face told me she couldn't either. We turned to see if he was still there and he was. He gently walked over to the front of the mirror, looked into it, and turned to look back at us again. He cast no reflection. He circled the mirror and replaced the cover.

He said, "That is why I no longer use mirrors. I could never see myself, even if I wanted to." Learchman just said, "Come with me." We followed without protest.

He led us to the conference room on the main level of the Manor. It was already eleven when we sat down with Learchman.

Emma reached across the table and held his hand, "Tell us William, tell us what's going on. Did you know that we, Tom and I have been in the mirrors?"

William nodded his head. "Yesterday? Yes, I didn't want you to get lost in there. It wasn't your first time."

Emma started, "We talked to the Changers. They told us that some of them got to come to our world, but only for a short time." She asked gently, "Are you one of them, William?"

"I'm not a Changer. Is that what you mean?

Through our conversation, we found that William Learchman was not slow witted or backward. He was surprisingly smart. Up until now, Learchman was a one sentence type of guy. He just listened most of the time. He would answer, generally with one word or maybe a couple. He began by telling us almost everything the Changer had told us. And a few things that he didn't.

He said, "You see, the changer told you that every time someone on this side is born, some one on that side is born also. Well that is somewhat true, sometimes they change. When someone here dies. . ." he paused a minute before continuing, "no one dies there. When someone dies here, their assigned roamer is ejected from the mirror world. He only has a split second to join his human. Did the changer tell you what happens when you meet your assigned roamer?

Probably not. Do you remember the Hub? Did it seem sort of confusing? All of the roamers there are the reflections of the people that no longer live here. If they were an assigned roamer, they simply continue to roam if they can't get out, always looking for their human. Did you see some of the roamers that never stopped at a window? They have no human."

Emma asked, "Are they cursed to roam for ever?" William let go of Emma's hand.

"Well not exactly," he continued, "Once they are ejected and if they miss that last second to connect with their human, they *are* destined to roam forever, on one side or the other. The one you spoke to in the hub was a controller. He has power that none of the others have. He can come into this world anytime he wants. He can bring anyone with him out of the mirrors or back in. He knows where all of the entrance mirrors are, and where all of the exit mirrors are as well. He can change a being's status on the other side, even do things for the people on this side. You see, as you learned tonight, just because you entered a mirror yesterday does not mean you can use it again tonight. A controller can do magical things. At least what *you* consider magical."

William went on, "If you think about it, if someone in the mirror can change your mood, or even change the way you look, well that would be magical, wouldn't it? So what if you had a dream? A dream so big it was impossible? And then you find a way to make it come true, do you do it? Of course you do. We have helped so many people. Since the beginning of human time, we've been around. We've made so many people smarter, happier, better and yes even on the negative side, we have, well, just let some people be, and not helped them at all. You know, some of the undesirables.

"When someone has a dream, and I mean a sleep type dream and they have an innovative idea the next day, where do you think that came from? Did you think that a person just went to sleep and woke up smarter? *We* put the answers in their head. *We* helped all of your historical figures become what they were.

Robert Slybeck was a fine student." He looked over to me, "You met his daughter, remember? Funny he never caught on to us, but we took him time after time to teach him things he had never even thought of. All of the great scientists, the mathematicians, the builders of your country. Tom Jefferson, Ben Franklin, Kennedy, Curie, and even Johnny J. Johnson.

Generally all of those people wake up in the morning and just think they figured out the problem from the night before or they begin to think of things they have never thought of before. Have you ever heard the term 'I'll sleep on it,' or 'let's sleep on it'? People say that because most people know subconsciously, of course, that they receive their inspirations at night. Sometimes they come to us and sometimes we go to them. Either way, life continually improves.

"When some of us come to this world, it's a better place for us, too! So to your question, Emma, am I a changer? No. I'm a Controller. I have control over this section of both worlds. I keep control of who goes in and who comes out. I am the one who controls Beddington.

"When you were in the mirrors, and at the hub, did you notice that the outside dimensions were not the same as the inside dimensions? Walter Beddington learned how to build like that. This Manor is built in the 4th dimension. We built it this way to accommodate many people and beings that transfer out of the mirrors. We had to have many rooms and a lot of space and yet the building had to look like it was just an old folks home from the outside."

"Walter stumbled into our mirrors over a hundred years ago, since then I was sent here by the Masters to keep things in control. I was here long before the beginning of the Manor.

My head was reeling. "The main changer, or the changer who we talked to said that you and your kind could only come here for a little while. So how is it that you and who knows how many others are here long term?" I wanted him to expose the others. "And none of you can cast a reflection? Is that true?"

William turned his eyes away from Emma and to me. "Yes, we really can stay here as long as there is no call for us in our world. And most of us are pretty sure there will be no call for us in our world." He looked over to Emma and then back to me. I just made the motion with my arms open and signaled 'why'.

He just said, "My human is dead, and I was too late." It only made sense that if any reflection that was not needed on the other side could come to this side from the mirror, then there could be millions of reflections on this side of the mirror.

I asked William, "How many people like you are here?"

He looked up from the table and stared directly at me and said, "Many."

William said, "It didn't start out this way. We used to only let a few Changers over here and only to help some of the humans that somehow found their way into the mirror. Like Walter."

I pressed, "So is it out of control?

William continued, "Once we figured out we could live here and be somewhat normal, and knowing if we stayed in the mirror, we would be forced to roam forever. We were naïve in . . ." his voice trailed off. He paused, looked down and said,

"Always looking for our human." After another long pause.

"They still are."

"There are thousands of Controllers like myself all over the world. It is my job to control this area. We don't let the Changers come now like we used to. It was always our purpose to help people. You know, to help them through their hours. We found a way to help ourselves too."

"Well it wouldn't be hard to find changers if they don't cast a reflection in a mirror," I said.

Learchman smiled, "They can cast a reflection, it just takes more energy. You see, in the mirror or outside of the mirror, the Changers do not get their energy from food. They get their energy from you and all of the people they are in contact with daily."

I protested, "But they can eat."

Learchman just said, "They can, but again, that is not where they get their energy. You may never see the assigned roamers who are here. The ones that missed their split second. You see, it is the controller's job to keep track of your hours. When your time is up, he is supposed to eject your roamer so he can connect. Many things can happen to disturb your time continuum."

"My what?" I said.

"Your life line. Your hours. If your roamer doesn't connect with you on your final second, he or she is doomed to roam forever.

Emma asked, "Is there anything else we should know, William?"

Learchman said, "Well, just one more thing. If they miss their chance to connect and are forced to roam your side, they are angry. You saw them change in the mirror? They can do the same thing on this side, too." He paused for a minute. "They can take the shape of anything."

I looked over to Emma and said, "I think we have a problem." The problem I referred to was not the changers or the roamers being here on our side of the mirror. The problem was no way to prove any of it.

Exhausted and overwhelmed, we said goodbye to Learchman at 4 a.m.

Chapter Twenty-One

It was a knock that woke me the next day. I lumbered out of bed and got to the door, and asked "Yes?"

The other side of the door just said, "Housecleaning."

"I'm still here, give me an hour or two." I glanced out the peephole and she was off without another word. On the other side of the bed were my notes from the night before. I gathered them up and placed them on the table by my laptop. I kept thinking about William talking in the plural. "We," "us, and "my human is dead" were words that kept spinning around in my head and on my notes as well. I began to think how many of these . . .beings are out there?

I went to the bathroom mirror and just stared at it for a while, wondering who else was behind the membrane watching *me*. Now all of a sudden I was becoming paranoid about the mirror. I pulled the drape to the shower before I removed my robe. I laughed at myself and my own paranoia.

The phone was ringing as I climbed out of the shower. I learned a long time ago that the phone would stop one second before I picked it up, so I never ran to the phone anymore. I figured it could only be Emma, who I would call pretty soon, and if it was anyone else, like the boss, I didn't want to talk to him, anyway.

I sat down to look over some of my notes, and began to type on the laptop. I only stopped to let the cleaning lady in and to order some lunch. I typed all day and no one else called and no other interruptions occurred. I forgot to call Emma, and because she didn't call me back, I figured she was working all day. When I realized the day was turning into night, and I was still in my robe, I hurriedly got dressed. I called the café and asked to talk to Emma.

"She just left," was the response. I called her house, but no answer.

A knock came at the door just as I hung up the phone. I checked the peephole and figured Emma must be a mind reader.

I opened the door, saying, "Hi Emma, I was just trying to call you." She entered and sauntered over to the table, which contained the remains of my lunch. I asked, "So how was your day?"

She stopped looking at the table and looked up at me, "You know what this means?" I was never good at guessing games and I hated this one even more. I was suppose to guess what she was talking about, and then guess what it meant.

I said, "What, what means?"

"Knowing the things we know," she retorted quite abruptly.

I could tell she was upset.

"You can't write that story, you know. I told you before, it will change lives, too many lives."

"Listen Emma, I have concluded that all of the residents of Beddington Manor were all beings, some human and some reflections of humans that have passed on. How to tell the difference is the trick.

"There is only one way to prove my theory. Take a mirror to Beddington Manor. If the residents could see themselves, obviously they were human. If they could not . . . well, you know."

"And what will that accomplish?" she asked.

"It will let us know what we are up against. Maybe none of those people are really people, have you ever thought of that? Maybe Mr. John Johnson is simply a reflection of the real Mr. Johnson." I probably spoke a little too loud. Emma looked away.

She said, "And what if my grandmother is . . .well, not my grandmother? I like the fact that I have a grandmother. I like the way things are. Tom, have you thought about the post office incident? I mean, maybe it's true. Maybe the time we spend looking into the mirror is subtracted from our lives. So what?

Maybe by not looking into a mirror, you don't get old as fast and maybe you can live longer. Who knows? But if you think you can take a mirror into Beddington and make all of those old folks look into it just to satisfy your curiosity, you're nuts, and I will not allow it. And even at the very worst, what if they all start to look their age and all the mirror changers and roamers and masters and all of that is just a bunch of bunk? You may be responsible for their deaths." She was fuming.

I said, "Their deaths? All I want them to do is look into a mirror."

She reminded me, "Tom, have you ever really known someone that is 122 years old? Even if he has not looked into a mirror in 70 years. And you have seen how frail my grandmother is, she has not looked into a mirror for over 50 years. What do you think she would look like if she actually carried all of those years? Not to mention Mr. Johnson." Emma's forehead relaxed and a smile crossed her face. She moved from the table toward me. She made eye contact and held the gaze as she moved.

"And besides, you know as well as I do, there is no one here to confirm your story. You don't want the whole world thinking you're nuts?" She continued her advance until she was just two inches from my face. "Do you?"

As I was staring into her eyes, she tilted her head to the side, closed her eyes and advanced the two inches that separated us. It was a longing satisfied that created another. We kissed quietly for a few seconds.

She backed off just little, but we were still wrapped up in each other. She raised her eyebrows, waiting for my answer.

I asked, "Well, do you think we could just talk to them one more time? Just to say good-bye? You know, thank them for their time and say good-bye. I have to say I am beginning to like Mr. Learchman."

Emma seemed unsure. "And what about your article? What are you going to put in your article?" I looked at all of my notes, "Well, the story really hasn't changed." The tightness of her arms loosened just a little, and her eyes widened. I went on, "Obviously I can't say that the building is built in the 4th dimension. I probably can't say anything about the mirrors. I will need to think about what I can say." Emma reach up and kissed me again, very soft and yet with a smile.

"Well, I came to meet the oldest man in the world," I said while she kissed me again, "I met him. He eats sensibly, he gets plenty of rest, plenty of exercise, and he has a very positive attitude. What more does the public need to know?" She kissed me again and noted her approval. "But we can go back, right?" I asked.

"You bet," was her response. The rest of the evening was spent in our own world without the mirrors or any thought of the previous night or current events.

The next morning I checked out of the Hotel. As we arrived at the Manor, William met us in the hallway.

"Are you okay?" he inquired. I was surprised by his question. "Are you here to go to the mirrors again?" I assured him we were only here to say good-bye to Mr. Johnson and Mrs. Brand. I told him I needed to get back home, as my work here was complete.

Beddington Manor

"And what will you write Mr. Benson?" I told him I was not sure exactly, but I would never talk or write of the other world. "No one would believe me, anyway."

We knocked on Clara Brand's door first. She came straight away and invited us in. We entered and sat down on the sofa.

She had that excited look on her face. "You know something, don't you? Something you didn't know before you got here."

Smiling, I said, "Mrs. Brand, I just came by to say good-bye. I need to be getting back to Denver. I really enjoyed our talks. Thank you, you're a wonderful lady."

Clara arose and left the room for a moment. She poked her head out of her room and motioned for me to come. I joined her in the bedroom. I could tell Clara had something in her hand. She said very low so Emma couldn't hear, "This is for you. This will answer all of your questions. Just take it and put it in your pocket. You'll figure it out later when you're alone." I took the box and placed it in my coat pocket.

We chatted a bit more and then Emma and I had to excuse ourselves to go and see Mr. Johnson.

On my way out, Clara gave me a little kiss on the cheek and said, "Mr. Benson, you're always welcome here. You're welcome to come back anytime." We were in the hallway and I faintly heard her say, "You'll be back."

Mr. Johnson met us at the bottom of the stairs. I called out "Hello Mr. Johnson, we were just coming to see you. I was just coming to say good-bye." I said it as if I would never see him again.

He picked that up saying, "When are you coming back? Are you going to write your article? If you write it, send me a copy." With that, he turned, not waiting for an answer, and disappeared down the hallway into his room.

I turned back to Emma and just gave a smile, "I think he will live forever. Let's see if we can find Learchman." We went down the first floor hallway and to the front desk. Mr. Learchman was there.

"Did you get to say your good-byes?" he asked. I told him we had seen Mr. Johnson and Miss Clara.

I said good-bye to William as he walked Emma and me out the front door. "You won't mind if I don't mention you in my story?" He just smiled, nodded and walked back to his front desk. "A man of few words," I said to Emma.

She laughed. "When *are* you coming back?" She asked.

I replied, "I thought I might talk you into coming to Denver for a while, maybe give the big city another chance. I could show you all the sites and it would be a lot of fun."

She gave me a kiss and said "Keep in touch, Tom Benson."

I could see her in the rear view mirror as I drove away, she was waving good-bye. In the mirror one second she was just waving and the next second it looked like she was trying to wave me back. I double checked and again she was just waving. I saw the Manor becoming smaller in the cars rearview mirror. I pulled off the road, stopped the car and adjusted the mirror to look at myself for minute. The eyes in the mirror were not mine.

I said to myself out loud, "Damm mirrors."

Chapter Twenty-Two

Again it was two hours from Twodot to the Helena airport. Leaving was harder than I thought it might be. Not only was it hard to say good-bye to Emma, I already knew I would miss William. In only a few days, I felt like I knew William, or at least getting to know him. I knew I had made some new friends and I knew I could come back to visit. I was still in a quandary as to what I was going to turn in to the 'Of Interest" publisher.

As I was driving, the past week kept going through my mind. I hoped I had all of the notes and files in order. I had most of the information on my laptop. I was so happy I put the 'trip to the mirrors' in the computer when it happened. I'm sure I would have forgotten it or thought it was a dream, just like Emma thought.

I arrived at the airport one hour ahead of schedule. Naturally the plane was late, so I had some extra time to reflect and re-read my notes. I pulled up my computer bag and pulled my notes from the side pocket. I began to read my notes about my confusion with the building itself. Smaller on the outside than on the inside? Well I knew the answer to this one, but could I tell it or not? Mr. Johnson really 122? A changer? Emma and I never really explored this possibility; however, it crossed my mind many times. I wondered about Mr. Johnson and Miss Clara and, quite frankly, I wondered about the truth for many of the residents of the Manor. How many were changers and how many were real people? After a person outlives all of his family, who would notice what happens to him or her?

If I wrote the true story, who would benefit and who could it hurt? I placed my jacket over my computer bag. As I did, a package fell out of the pocket. Ah, this was the package that Clara gave to me. I forgot about it until now. "This will answer all of your questions" she had said. I opened the box and found a pair of old, old spectacles. I thought, what was she thinking? These must have been her husband's glasses. However, they were in very good shape. I lifted them to my eyes and removed them again very fast. I couldn't believe what I saw.

I lifted the glasses again to my face to see some of the people in the airport surrounded by roamers. It looked like almost every person in the airport had two or three or four roamers right next to them. I placed the glasses on my nose so that I could see above and through them. The glasses didn't answer my questions. And now I had even more. Each person looked like a crowd. I could see through the glasses that the roamers were talking and yelling in silence at the human they enclosed.

I removed the glasses and placed them back in their case. All again appeared normal. I secured the case inside my computer bag and locked the pocket. These glasses, of course were not ordinary glasses. I doubted they had belonged to Clara's husband and I had no idea why she gave them to me, but now that I had them I felt obligated to tell the whole truth. The truth about how these people could possibly live so long. The truth about the mirrors. The million hours. . . boy, that was a big one. I had to think about that one. There were so many variables that it was almost impossible to figure how many hours anyone had left to live. I mean, if you subtracted your sleeping hours from the equation or at least your sleeping hours when you slept in a room that did not contain any mirrors. . . Of course you had to double the hours that included any bad habits or anything that could have had a negative effect on your life. I wondered if that included stress or my time in rush hour traffic. And what about the time I was in a room with a mirror, but was not looking into the mirror? And how about when I was twelve and went to the local amusement park and spent hours in the hall of mirrors? When there are multiple reflections, does that add all of that time for each reflection? It was so confusing, I hesitated to try to figure how much time I had left.

I had to re-evaluate my priorities and my values. I had the proof right here in my computer bag. These glasses proved that we deal with the mirror people each and every day, and now I learned that we deal with them whether we are in front of a mirror or not. They weren't like Learchman. Here to do a job, to make someone's life better? I was convinced their motivation was not honorable.

So here I sit with a moral dilemma. I could tell all and probably be hauled off to the loony bin. I am sure there would be very few believers. Again I had to decide who would be hurt and who would be helped by this knowledge.

Emma was right: lives would change if I wrote this story. This was the first time I had to weigh the pros and cons of the delivery of a story. I always said, "Tell it like it is, and let the readers decide on the validity of the story." Some would laugh and just blow it off and some might call the magazine and complain. There would be, however, some people that would believe the story just the way it was written. What would I do with those folks? They would come to me with the questions. What would I say? I had to break it down to what I knew and what I could say.

Chapter Twenty-Three

I knew I could write a great story about John Johnson. I knew he was born in 1880 in New York City. He was the 9th of 11 children. He graduated from Princeton in 1906. His father was a doctor and Johnny followed in his dad's path along with three of his brothers. He did his internship in Mercy Medical and joined the Family practice in 1910. Johnny met the love of his life in 1911, Lenora Prescott. They were married just 1 year later. Mr. Johnson and Lenora raised 14 children and during their adulthood, have all scattered throughout the United States.

Johnny and Lenora spent a few years in Denver, Colorado and were lured away from there by an old family friend, Walter Beddington. Walter had been friends with Johnny's father and went West years earlier to start a settlement, which he named Beddington. Walter Beddington had many people moving into his new settlement. The one thing he did not have was a doctor. He contacted Mr. Johnson and persuaded him to join the settlement in Montana. With the population growing and always wanting to go west, Johnny and Lenora decided it was the right time to have their own practice, even if it was in Montana.

Walter and Johnny were instrumental in building the first Hospital in Beddington. Finally, not only did Johnny have his own practice, he was the director of the Hospital and was responsible for all of the medical needs for all of the citizens of the city.

Most of Johnny and Lenora's children were born in that very hospital. Lenora, without any medical training, worked every day in the hospital. There was always something to do and something to take care of.

Up until his retirement in 1950, he had delivered just about every baby that was born in this county and most of the other neighboring counties as well. Dr. Johnson learned a long time ago that he needed to stay fit and eat right.

He told me that he has been retired for over 50 years, so I didn't need to call him Dr. Johnson anymore.

When I asked him the secret to his longevity, he simply said, "I just keep waking up every morning and I keep taking air. Maybe it's just something in the water. So as long as I can still take nourishment and air, I guess I will just hang around. And when it is my hour to go, I will go."

Mr. Johnson and a number of the other residents of the retirement home he resides in were tested recently for the old age gene. According to the hospital that did the testing, some of the people had it and some did not. There was a higher concentration of the gene in this area than in some others.

Results; inconclusive.

I couldn't get past the word inconclusive. I thought the entire trip, the entire week was inconclusive. I knew I couldn't leave here with so many loose ends dangling. I knew I needed more information. Mr. Johnson was correct, he said some people like me just kept coming back. I was compelled to go back. And now that I had these glasses. . . Clara was wrong, the glasses didn't answer all of my questions, they sparked more and more questions that needed to be answered. I canceled my flight, re-rented a car and headed back to Twodot.

Chapter Twenty-Four

I was anxious to get back to Beddington. I didn't stop at Paradise or even the café in Twodot. I went directly to the Manor. As I was driving up to the front of the Manor, the front didn't look the same as when I left just this morning. I had the glasses in my pocket and walked up the steps to the front door. I could see the screen door was missing. The door was ajar. I entered, the hallway was dark. Dust and cobwebs everywhere. I wandered down the hallway a little, no sign of anyone. No Learchman, no residents, no one on the first floor. I went up the staircase and directly to Clara's room. The door was closed, I knocked. There was no answer. I twisted the door knob, it was unlocked. I walked into her room to find all of the same furniture I had just sat on this morning was in a shamble. Dust, dirt and cobwebs all over the place. It looked like no one had been here for years. I returned to the dresser that didn't have the mirror that Clara had been staring into after our first meeting. I turned the top of the dresser around to see the mirror frame, it was blank. I began to doubt that the past seven days even occurred. The one solace for me was that the windows were still covered with muslin.

As I returned to the main floor, I entered Mr. Johnson's apartment. It was in the same condition as Clara's. I immediately entered his restroom. The picture of Mr. Johnson that had been mounted where the mirror was supposed to be was no longer hanging in its place. A mirror frame was there, however, no mirror.

I returned to the hallway. I pulled the glasses from my pocket. As I put them on, the other world came to life. Everything was clean and shining again. I could see people walking down the hallway. I was about to talk to one of them, when I noticed Emma coming toward me. I looked over the top of the glasses and all was empty again, except for Emma. She was still walking to me. I looked up again and I could see the good side of the Manor and Emma was still there. Once I removed the glasses, Emma and I were the only ones there. I placed the glasses in their case before she spoke.

"Hi Tom, you came back." She stopped with that and didn't offer any explanation.

"Emma," I said, "What is this?" I said as I motioned with my hands upraised to emphasize the Manor.

She began, "This is how the Manor really looks. It seems every now and again, the Controllers allow some outsiders in. Sometimes, some people get a glimpse of the other world. That is what you got, Tom. Since you arrived in Twodot, who have you talked to besides me?"

I had to think about it, "Well, you know I have talked to Clara and Mr. Johnson and Mr. Learchman. I also talked to one of the maids at the hotel."

Emma asked, "Did you have a conversation with the maid?"

I had to think and of course I didn't. So I had to say

"No."

"Why did you come back, Tom?" She continued. "Do you remember when Mr. Johnson said, 'some people like you just keep coming back'? I nodded my head. She answered for me, "Maybe that's why you're here?"

I reached for my pocket and said, "The glasses. I mean, I was at the airport in Helena and the package that Clara gave me fell out of my jacket pocket. I opened it up and saw the glasses. I put them on and the airport blossomed with see-through roamers. This is the proof. This is the proof that Changers and roamers are all around us."

Emma just smiled, "The glasses that Clara gave you, they don't really change anything."

I protested, "Well once I put them on, a lot of people came out of nowhere." She corrected and asked,

"And when you took them off, did those see-through people disappear? Were any of the people in the airport affected by the roamers?"

I had to confess, "Well everything appeared to be normal, once I removed the glasses."

She continued, "And here, what happened when you put them on?"

Confused I stammered, "Well no, I mean there was nothing here until I put them on. Then everything was back to normal." I looked at the glasses and asked, "How does that work?"

Emma explained, "Tom, you have been given a great gift."

"Oh yes, the glasses, I just don't know how to work 'em."

Emma said, "No, the glasses are just a tool to use the gift. The gift it being able to see the truth. People generally go through their life seeing things any way they want to see it. You, as a reporter, should know this all too well.

"Have you ever received the same story from two eyewitnesses of the same event? Are the two stories ever the same? How could two or more people see the same event and yet each person came out with a different version of it? It is because they all see the event from a different angle or perspective?"

I found myself mesmerized by Emma again. She had a way of holding me with every sentence and word.

"You," she went on, "have the power to see the truth. The glasses are simply a tool you can use to help you see it. Never doubt the truth. The changers and the roamers are real, but they are not going to expose the truth to everyone. Some are just going to have to believe.

"Do you remember when William said the roamers that missed their split second to connect were angry?"

"Well, yes of course. I thought they were the ones inside the mirrors who roamed each window and never stopped." I said.

"Don't you think that some of the roamers are in this world as well? They are. They are looking for a new connection. Otherwise they are cursed to roam forever. The ones on the other side were sucked in by the mirror and will never have a chance to move to the next level.

"Oh Tom, if you ever need an answer, look to the mirrors."

As Emma was talking, I opened the case the glasses were in and removed them to put them back on. As I looked up, I was surrounded by mirrors. Emma cast no reflection. She stepped into the mirror right in front of me. She turned back to me and threw a kiss and then disappeared into the mirror. I quickly turned to see if I could see her in any of the other mirrors. She was gone. I put my hand up to the mirror she had vanished into, and the door was shut. I could not follow or enter the mirror. I touched all of the mirrors that reflected me, to no avail.

As I drove away from the dilapidated Manor, the only thing I saw in the car rearview mirror was the building. The way everyone saw it. Old and dilapidated.

Chapter Twenty-Five

I arrived at the Denver Airport and had planned to take a cab home. To my surprise, Kate Slybeck was waiting for me at the gate. I said, Hello Kate.

She reached out to shake my hand, "Hello Tom. Did you find what you were looking for?"

"I found much more than I was ever looking for. What brings you to the airport?"

"You Tom." She smiled.

"And how did you know which gate I would be at?"

"I have my ways."

We began to walk down the concourse together. As we passed one of the little stores in the center of the airport, I asked, "could you come with me for just a second?" She nodded and followed me into the clothing shop. I led her to the rear of the store and we both stopped in front of the mirror.

Once we stopped, she smiled through the mirror and said, "Yes, I'm real."

"Just checking," I said, as we returned to the concourse. "Do you have a car here?"

"Follow me." She said.

I returned to my office in Denver the next day.

Here's what I wrote for the Magazine:

It must be in the Water!

By Tom Benson

Article Pending
(the rest of the page is blank)

_____

I sent a card and a copy of the magazine with no article on Beddington to Mr. Johnson and a copy to Emma.

In Emma's copy, I wrote "Emma, let me know when you can come to Denver."

I never heard back.

I still plan to go back some time to see all of my friends in Twodot. Beddington will be my choice for my retirement home. . .when I'm ready.

Jack Shyrer said it was the biggest waste of time that he had ever seen. During my review of the story with him, I noticed the picture he was holding when he gave me the assignment. It was a 5x7 black and white of Mr. Johnson. The same picture that appeared in the newspaper just three weeks ago, wishing Mr. Johnson a birthday wish. Jack never mentioned the picture, but seemed very disappointed that I had less of a story than he expected. He said 'Article pending' was unacceptable and I needed to complete the report on Mr. Johnson.

He gave me a temporary assignment until my story was finished.

He decided I could help the copy editor. I would be going over some of the reports that were sent in by other reporters. He said I needed to get off the street for a while.

Oh, the glasses? I still have them!

THE END

Closing Thoughts

Thanks for taking the time to read this book. This is my first effort for a complete book. I have always had a fascination for mirrors. I have always thought there was more going on there than met the eye.

When I was young I always thought I could see people in the mirrors. I figured that if I tried hard enough, I could visit them. I would stand and stare at a mirror for hours. I would have conversations with these people regularly. I used the mirrors for an escape from reality.

Consequently, I had a very easy time getting through school. Now that I think about it, maybe some of those conversations did help me. Who knows?

In my adult life, I always thought my reflection ate more than I did, because every time I looked into the mirror, he was heavier. He still is.

I don't talk to the people in the mirrors any more. Well, not too much. At least that I can remember.

Any way, I hope you enjoyed the story, and again, thanks.

Feel free to e-mail me and let me know how you liked the book, or let me know what you didn't like.

All feedback is welcome

Thanks again,

Kelly Haglund
khaglund9975@msn.com